IRREGULAR
PEOPLE

Janet Fehr

Preface

This is a book about people. Some are irregular, some are not. Some are handicapped, some are not. But everyone one of them is important and has a place on the master blueprint.

This book is also about story telling. A story is a story, but the way it is told determines whether you listen, or read to the end, or give up halfway out of sheer boredom.

I am a story teller, and my view of life is slightly off centre, perhaps because unusual things happen to me. Or maybe the things that happen to me are ordinary, and I am off centre, making my perception of everything appear unusual. Then again, it could be that I am ordinary and the things that happen to me are ordinary, and it is only the story teller in me that makes these things seem extraordinary.

Whatever the case, the first two stories will give you an inkling as to my character, and how I spin my tales. Then it's up to you whether or not to read the rest of the book.

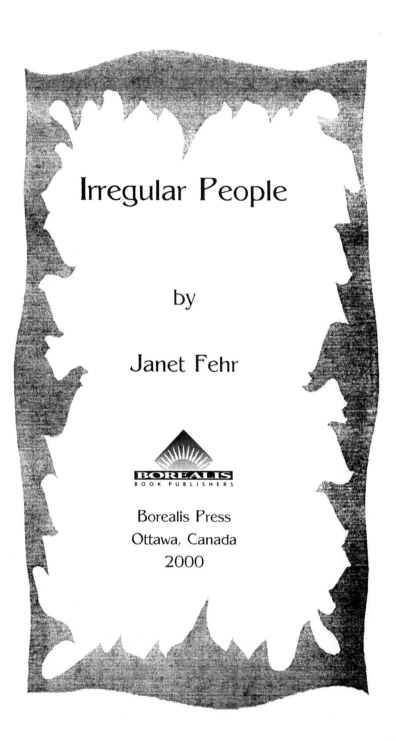

Irregular People

by

Janet Fehr

BOREALIS
BOOK PUBLISHERS

Borealis Press
Ottawa, Canada
2000

We acknowledge the financial support of the Government of Canada through the Book Publishing Industry Development Program (BPIDP), for our publishing activities.

Canadian Cataloguing in Publication Data

Fehr, Janet, 1942-
    Irregular people

Short stories.
ISBN 0-88887-236-4 (bound) - ISBN 0-8887-238–0 (pbk.)

    I Title.

PS8561.E355I77 2000   C813'.6   C00-900735-0
PR9199.3.F43I77 2000

Cover by Bull's Eye Design, Ottawa;

Printed and bound in Canada on acid-free paper.

Contents

1   Introduction 1

2   The Long Dark Night 7

3   False Dawn 32

4   Sunrise 85

5   Us And Them 95

The opinions expressed in these stories are those of the author and do not reflect those of any individuals or organizations.

All names except the author's have been changed, and some circumstances have been altered.

1

Introduction

No Babinski

One Thanksgiving weekend when I was a student at university, I went home with my roommate to spend the holiday with her family. They lived on the edge of a small farming community with an uncleared area of trees, undergrowth, and vague game trails just back of their yard. Drawn by the magnificent colors and pungent smells of autumn, I decided to explore the trails.

The crisp northern air gave me the kind of high only John Denver and lovers of the outdoors can appreciate, and I carefully bent under tree branches and stepped over exposed roots as I picked my way through the miniature forest. Dry leaves crunched under my feet and stones rolled in my wake and I forgot the city and my studies in the cool calmness of the autumn sunshine.

As I turned to make the hike back, I did one of the things I do best. I stumbled over my own foot and crashed to the ground, striking my head on a rock as I landed. I got up and dusted myself off, not realizing that I had knocked myself out for a brief period of time. Blissfully ignorant, I wandered back along a different trail, emerging from the wood at an unfamiliar fence, and an unknown house and yard on the other side.

Undaunted, I climbed the fence, a chicken-wire affair, and as I raised one leg over the top, I lost consciousness and hung dangling by my other leg for God knows how long.

Things became fuzzy after that. I don't recall untangling myself, but I do remember falling face down a couple of times in a heavenly cool, lush lawn before deciding that I would just stay there forever. After a time I roused myself and was immediately restrained by a cool hand on my neck and a female voice insisting that I lie still because she couldn't find my pulse. I remember thinking what an odd statement since if I was moving I must have a beating heart. Then I opened my eyes and beheld the most curious thing I had ever seen. A woman was kneeling beside me with two small children hovering behind her. It was difficult to determine their concern, or lack of it, because I was seeing everything like the negative of a photograph.

I blinked my eyes and thought how strange it all was, then opened them and looked again. Colors sprang out at me, positive and beautiful, and I struggled up out of the cool grass, feeling clumsy and foolish.

A doctor in the town's tiny hospital gave me a pill for headaches (if I got one) and a capsule for nausea (if I felt it) and sent me home to my roommate's family for Thanksgiving dinner. Later, we piled into the car for the long drive back to the city and school.

Upon arrival, however, I found I could not exit the car because my left leg would not work. A ninety-degree bend at the knee refused to straighten out, and any attempt to do so produced excruciating pain. The next day I hobbled into the Emergency Student Health Clinic on campus, sure in the knowledge that the only course of action was amputation. I tried to be positive by reflecting that I had not suffered a headache or nausea, which would seriously have complicated the situation.

A female intern who looked young and inexperienced nervously examined my knee, then asked how it had happened. I explained that I didn't know because I thought I had fallen and hit my head. Immediately she seized upon the head injury, finding it infinitely more interesting than a knee that refused to unbend.

She kneaded my scalp, probed my ears, shone a light in my eyes, and flopped me back and forth on an x-ray table taking pictures of my head, totally unmindful of the crippling pain in my knee each time she demanded I move. Finally she got around to checking my reflexes and when she tapped my tortured knee with her little hammer, I was transported to a new plateau of pain.

She committed a final indignity by removing my shoes and socks and drawing her thumbnail along the length of the soles of my feet. I was beginning to understand how lab animals felt. Again the thumb on the soles of my feet. A puzzled look filled her countenance, and then a flush of excitement.

"You have no Babinski," she proclaimed, the diagnostician in her elated at the insight.

"So?" I queried.

"That means you're retarded." She replied, apparently appalled by my ignorance.

"But I'm a student here at university," I protested wildly.

"That's amazing," she mused, "simply amazing. A retard attending university!" And her eyes glazed over as if she had made some medical breakthrough worthy of the Nobel Prize.

It was later determined that I had, in fact, suffered a moderate concussion in my original fall, and had sustained torn ligaments in my knee when I hung, unconscious, on the fence.

And yes, I have no Babinski reflex, but no, I am not retarded, at least not in the clinical sense!

A Regular Mom

My father, though poorly educated, had a passion for words. He loved books, and as I grew up we read together and amused ourselves with word games that we invented and re-invented and perfected on an almost daily basis. I did the same with my child. Whereas the activity was immensely satisfying for my dad and I, the word games were a constant source of frustration for my daughter, for along with my clumsiness and lack of Babinski reflex, I did not fit the accepted parameters of mother, as determined by her.

This didn't bother me too much, because I didn't fit the parameters of anything, and aside from the occasional bump on the head, or torn knee ligaments, I had managed admirably. One day, when she was about eight years old, my daughter came home from school and interrupted a conversation I was having with Michael, our dog. I talked to him all the time like he was a person and I was in my right mind. My child looked at me and the dog, and heaved a sigh that was laden with the cares of the world.

"Hi, Twit-faced Kid," I said brightly, "what's the problem?"

"I have a name, you know, Mother," and she sighed again in desperation.

"That's a problem?" I replied, and patting Michael's furry brow, commented, "we'll finish talking later."

"No, Mother," she threw up her hands, "the problem is you. I come home and you're talking philosophy with the dog! You play the air guitar while you're getting supper ready! You wear dresses made out of old bed sheets! And you cook broccoli and carrots for me all the time!"

Her accusations stung me, but they were all true.

She passionately concluded with, "If only you were a regular mom!"

Ahah! She had given the cue! "As opposed to an irregular mom?" I asked, pleased with my opening gambit in our endless word game.

Exasperated, she stomped out of the kitchen and down the hall to her room. Hitching up my bedsheet dress and tripping over Michael, I followed her, realizing the game was out of the question, but curious about regular moms.

"So tell me," I demanded, "what is a regular mom? Give me an example of one."

"You're not. Melissa's mom is," came the clipped reply, making me proud of her command of words.

I dropped my bedsheet skirt and pondered. Here was food for thought.

Melissa's mom was a neighbour; a quiet, petite, pretty woman with a luxurious head of sun-blond hair. She was a pleasant person who helped me from time to time with the Brownie pack to which my daughter and Melissa belonged. I pondered more. Some things are beyond human capabilities. I was tall and awkward, and could be quiet, perhaps, if I was gagged and drugged. Pretty was totally out of the picture, but blond, now there was something I could work with, given the right hair stylist and a bottle of peroxide.

"I could bleach my hair," I shouted at my daughter as her bedroom door slammed shut.

"Forget it, Mom, you're hopeless," came her muffled reply.

I went back to Michael, and together we hatched a plan.

It took my perceptive child nearly a week to notice that things were not the way they had always been. She was almost solicitous when she asked me one evening if I was okay. I assured her I was fine as I quietly washed the supper dishes.

"You're sure there's nothing wrong?" she persisted.

I adjusted my apron, smoothed my shirt, and straightened my jeans. "I'm great," I replied, "what makes you think anything is wrong?"

She narrowed her eyes and peered up at me. "Well, you've been real quiet lately, you're not dressing weird, you haven't talked to Michael in a week, and your hair's got blond streaks in it. Are you sick, Mom?"

"Nope," I said, "just being a regular mom."

My twit-faced kid then groaned, rolled her eyes, and burst out laughing. "Well, I don't like it," she gasped between guffaws, "it's not normal for you. You were better when you were an irregular mom. But you can keep the blond streaks. Those I like!""

"Thank you!" I shouted, and picked her up and hugged her and swung her around the kitchen. Then I set her down, and immediately broke into song, accompanied by my long-necked, left-handed air guitar. The commotion drew Michael and my husband from the livingroom, and they gaped at us from the kitchen door as we giggled and pranced around the room.

Four or five years later, on a blustery Christmas Eve, Melissa's mom apparently became weary of her regular life, and attempted suicide. Unfortunately, she botched it, and now lives in a place with other brain-damaged folk, waiting for someone to comb the tangles out of her sun-blond hair and tell her when to go to the bathroom.

Lucky for me I was an irregular mom!

Recently, my now-adult daughter explained to me what her definition of a regular mom was when she was seven years old. It was someone who could make juicy Kraft Dinner the way Melissa's mom did it.

Fat chance. I don't like Kraft Dinner, juicy or otherwise.

2

The Long Dark Night

Historians will argue that without a clear understanding of the past, the present is chaos, and the future is questionable. History takes on a totally new dimension when you are part of it. And I was part of the history of rehabilitation services in Canada. Daily events that seemed unremarkable became significant in retrospect, and it is only when I look back and remember can I begin to understand the impact of those events on what I do today, and what I may attempt tomorrow.

Societal attitudes towards persons who are handicapped are as diverse as the people who form society. And societal attitudes have shaped and directed the history of persons who are handicapped. For the most part it is a grim history, filled with pain and written with tears of frustration. There has been incredible fear, shame and misunderstanding, and there has been humor. The ignorance of some has been appalling; the insight of others, inspiring.

In the pages that follow, there are stories that must be told, whether we want to hear them or not, for it is only through this process can we hope to emerge from the long dark night into the radiance of the sunrise.

The Thirties

*The years between 1930 and 1939 are not fondly
remembered by many. It was a desperate time. People
watched the wind blow their lives away as they waited
and prayed for rain. The Dirty Thirties gave birth to
survival skills never before dreamed of.*

*Franklin Delano Roosevelt believed the only thing we
had to fear was fear itself. Adolf Hitler was made the
Chancellor of Germany, and another fear stirred. King
Edward VIII made the ultimate sacrifice, abdicating the
throne of England and marrying for love, something
apparently unheard of in royal history. A talented young
animator named Disney transformed the fairy tale, Snow
White into a classic movie that would delight generations of children. And a black man named Jessie Owens
became an Olympic hero.*

*A wonder drug derived from a common mold sent a
thrill of excitement through the medical community as
penicillin was used to attack and vanquish all manner of
infections.*

*William Faulkner, a little known author, penned <u>The
Sound and The Fury.</u> His writing had an odd style which
was difficult to read, but the subject matter was unmis-
takable. The story was about a 33-year-old man-child
who was born loony, hidden away and cared for by his
family. Faulkner borrowed his title from William Shake-
speare who wrote that life was "full of sound and fury,
signifying nothing," which was the implied attitude
towards the character in the book.*

In a dusty, windswept prairie town, in the middle of
the Dirty Thirties, a young registered nurse, newly graduated and filled with vision, was struggling to survive
in a tiny hospital that could barely support the nuns who
operated it. She was a good nurse, quick and efficient,

trusted by the doctors because she had the uncanny ability to anticipate their needs in surgery and in the case room, where babies were delivered.

It was a time when doctors and nurses were frequently paid with freshly butchered chickens, baskets of garden produce, or a couple of dozen farm eggs simply because farmers had little money and weren't going to waste it on medical care.

One day the drama of survival fell on this young nurse's shoulders and wrapped her in a dark cloak of fear and uncertainty. A farm wife was brought to the hospital, well into hard labor. She was wheeled into the case room, leaving her husband and children hovering anxiously in the waiting room. She might have been young and attractive, but it was difficult to tell with having to care for several young ones at home, and work beside her husband on a farm that was daily being eroded by the relentless wind.

Her face was covered with a sheen of sweat, and her features were grim and determined as the contractions wracked her tired body. The doctor and young nurse worked together until the child slipped out of its protective cocoon and the mother drifted off into exhausted slumber.

The doctor held the baby and instructed the nurse to cut the cord. He then handed it over to her and told her to set it aside while they tended to the mother. The young nurse took the child and immediately recognized that it was malformed and probably retarded. At the same instant, she realized the implication of the doctor's orders. If the umbilical cord was not clamped, the child would bleed to death.

She laid the infant down and turned to the doctor, whose eyes told her no questions were to be asked because he had made his decision regarding that tiny life.

The woman and her family were told by the doctor that the baby had been stillborn, which was indeed a blessing because it was a monstrosity. Had it lived, it would have been an incredible burden on them, and society.

The Forties

The forties was a decade of extremes. Hitler's insanity burned white hot as the world was forced to endure the horror of the holocaust. Incredibly, physicists achieved the first controlled nuclear chain reaction, and the depravity in Europe was matched by the devastation of the bombs dropped on Hiroshima and Nagasaki. How was anyone to know that generations after Japan had recovered and rebuilt, the grim legacy of those bombs would appear and reappear in malformed and diseased babies?

But then the war was over. The baby boomers were born, and the world would never be quite the same. People got high on peace. They had just come through the war to end all wars. It couldn't happen again.

A medical breakthrough was responsible for isolating the molecular flaw which caused sickle cell anemia in American blacks, bringing hope to those suffering from the terrible pain of that disease.

John Steinbeck, a tall, thoughtful man, wrote the first of several books. It, along with his others, forced readers to search their souls for understanding and compassion. Of Mice and Men was beautifully written, easy to read, and deceptively short. It told the story of Lennie: "a giant working machine who wasn't too bright; he could take orders; he was dumb as hell."

Lennie's friend George looked out for him because he didn't want him sent to the "booby hatch where they'd put a collar on him and tie him up like a dog." But in the end it was his friend George who shot him like a dog, in the back of the head, because Lennie's brute strength had combined with his curiosity to betray him. George truly believed he was doing the right thing for Lennie.

Steinbeck clearly understood the depth of fear that could be felt of someone who was different, and the breadth of prejudice that naturally sprang from such great fear.

I grew up in a small town that bordered on sprawling farmlands to the south and magnificent lakes and forests to the north. It was a busy community, large enough to support prosperous enterprise, small enough that people knew each other well, accepting the eccentricities of their fellow citizens.

There were the Calcimine Twins, a pair of elderly, widowed sisters who painted themselves up with their powder and lipstick, dressed themselves in their ensembles including white gloves and hats, and daily meandered through town like dowager queens surveying their kingdom.

There was the wrinkled, leathery old Indian woman who could have been seventy or a hundred and seventy, but whose reputation was based on rock-solid fact. She had operated an extremely successful cat house and in her heyday had used her profits to open an equally successful car dealership in town. According to the story, she was motivated to go into business because she tried to pay cash for a new car from the only dealership in town, and the owner refused to take her money!

There was the very proper, stiff-upper-lipped English doctor who never abandoned the British habit of serving supper at nine o'clock in the evening. Those invited to dine with he and his family knew enough to eat before they went so as not to faint dead away waiting for supper to be served.

And there was Teddy. His origins were obscure, as was his age. He was just always there. He presented no threat. He was well-mannered, clean-shaven, and smelled faintly of bar sunlight soap. He could read a little, and he was a hard worker. Teddy swept sidewalks downtown in the summer, and shoveled snow in the winter. He unloaded inventory and kept stockrooms tidy. He made deliveries and assisted shop keepers with minor building repairs. He was employed by nearly everyone in town, and he paid rent, bought groceries and clothed himself with the money he made.

On more than one occasion he assisted me with my bicycle chain when I got a pant leg caught and stood trapped unable to free myself. I recall that he was of average size and build, and he spoke clearly enough that everyone could understand him. His face was always wrapped up in an enormous smile and he stood ready at all times to do what was asked of him, or to help someone who needed assistance.

Though no one ever said so, it was clearly understood that Teddy was the town idiot, just one of the many characters woven into the fabric of our community. Looking back, it appears his life was untroubled: no stress, no pressures, just daily odd jobs, a hot meal and a warm, comfortable bed at night.

That small town of my childhood has grown and prospered, and all those characters have long since disappeared, including Teddy. The beauty and simplicity of his life was demonstrated by the ease with which he was accepted by the people of my town, and the void left with his passing.

The Fifties

The years between 1950 and 1959 meandered smoothly and lazily like a quiet stream after the white water of the forties. There were stretches of urgent currents and swirling eddies, but it was, overall, a tranquil passage.

Polio swept in and sent rip tides of fear through the hearts of baby boom parents, until Dr. Salk turned the tide with his life-saving vaccine. Science and medicine combined to assist women seeking relief from the discomforts of pregnancy, but the reality of that help became a tragedy when the thalidomide babies were born with shortened upper limbs, flipper-like hands, and in some cases, no arms at all.

The man, who in the thirties gave the world Snow White, created a paradise of fun for children and parents alike, and named it after himself: Disneyland. The Russians introduced the world to the reality of space travel with their launching of Sputnik. Color television, while financially out of reach for many, mystified all in much the same manner as the earlier black and white version had done.

The incredibly prolific imagination of Dr. Seuss began its journey through children's literature with <u>The Cat In a Hat</u>, and a Canadian woman dared to write a book about a subject that throughout the history of persons with disabilities has fueled debates which often become apoplectic shouting matches.

The book was titled <u>The Light in the Piazza</u>, and the subject was marriage. The heroine was Clara, a lovely young woman brain-damaged at the age of ten due to an unfortunate accident. The hero was a hot-blooded Italian who fell in love with her simplicity and unaffected approach to life. Clara is referred to in the book as a child who never grew up, an unfortunate parallel that has *survived the decades.*

The marriage is supported by Clara's mother, although her motive for doing so is unclear. Is she simply weary of caring for a child in an adult's body, or does she genuinely hope for a degree of happiness and fulfillment for her daughter? Or would marriage make her more "normal," thereby guaranteeing her acceptance by a society that looked upon her as retarded?

In the real world of an institution that housed fifteen hundred men, women and children who had multiple handicaps, the common denominator being mental retardation, an inexperienced dietetic aide was struggling to keep her breakfast down. Her senses had never been so assaulted by the smells, sounds and sights she now experienced. The things she saw so upset her internal balance that eating was a near impossibility, and keeping any food down took a monumental effort.

Fortunately, after several weeks on the job she became immune to the pseudo-antiseptic stench of the place, and the clangor and clatter of a thousand voices was tuned out as she tried to make sense of the things she saw.

Her duties frequently took her from the bustle of the main kitchen to the slower, quieter satellite sculleries of the institution. She worked several shifts in the infirmary and was calmed by its serene, unhurried atmosphere. The infirmary housed incoming individuals during a quarantine period. Primarily they were checked for communicable diseases, but they were also assessed for intellectual and behavioral status, resulting in their assignment to an appropriate ward or cottage. There were seldom more than one or two people in the infirmary at any given time, so the kitchen duties were light.

When the dietetic aide wasn't busy she liked to pass the time chatting with the nursing staff, or the trainees serving their quarantine. One day a new arrival caught her eye. He looked about four years old, with a thick mop of unruly blond hair, and his blue eyes sparkled with mischief as he padded around the ward in striped pyjamas, a fuzzy bathrobe, and slippers with bobbing bunnies on the toes. He smiled easily and laughed frequently, and had the insatiable curiosity of most children his age.

The aide wondered what he was doing there. Because of her inexperience, she missed the slanted eyes with the mongolian fold. She also failed to notice that the bridge of his nose was somewhat flattened, and although his tongue seemed a little larger than normal, his speech was totally unaffected. In fact, he prattled endlessly about his new environment. His hands were short and broad, but so was the rest of him: he was a stocky four-year-old.

The curious kitchen worker finally asked one of the nurses about him.

"He's a mongoloid idiot," she was told, "a classic example of that specific form of mental retardation. He'll probably only live till he's twenty or twenty-five. His parents tried to keep him at home, but they just couldn't cope, so we've got him now."

The young woman was appalled.

"But he's so bright and cute and friendly," she protested. "How could anyone just give him up?"

The nurse shook her head. "Don't be fooled by appearances," she explained. "There's no doubt he's retarded. This is the best place for him, with his own kind."

The child in this story had Down Syndrome. The chilling post script to this tale is the possibility that he may have been a mosaic: one of a few variants that have barely recognizable clinical signs of Down Syndrome, but with average intelligence!

The Sixties

The placid waters of the fifties exploded over an endless, tortured waterfall as the unsuspecting world moved into the years between 1960 and 1969.

The decade began with the construction of the Berlin Wall, dividing a city and a nation of people not yet fully recovered from Hitler's madness. Then, reeling from the assassination of John F. Kennedy, we were hurled into the Vietnam War. Suddenly and inexplicably, another Kennedy was slain. The civil rights movement gathered momentum behind its powerful leader, but Martin Luther King also fell to an assassin's bullet.

The uninhibited violence of the sixties was balanced by two wondrous events: the landing of American astronauts on the moon, and the first human heart transplant by a South African surgeon.

The world of the arts gave us an unusual book, <u>Flowers For Algernon</u>, which Hollywood later turned into the movie, <u>Charlie</u>, starring Cliff Robertson. It is the story of a retarded man who becomes a genius through the efforts of medical science. Sadly, the transformation was only temporary, and as quickly as his intellectual superiority soared, Charlie crashed back to his "subhuman" state, with little or no memory of his experience. The book is pure science fiction, but there is a haunting message. Charlie discovered that public acceptance of him was consistent. He was ostracized, both as an idiot and a genius. If there was a difference, he concluded, it was that when he was retarded he was happy. Even his induced superior intelligence could give him no understanding of why people were so frightened by him.

In the sixties there seemed to be a heightened public awareness of persons who were handicapped, but that awareness was sadly lacking in humanity. Individuals who were mentally handicapped were referred to as mongoloids, retardates, sub-humans, idiot babies, and occasionally seen as gifted or deprived by those wanting to appear less judgmental or more charitable. The decade of the sixties was truly a dark time, but there was the occasional flicker of humor.

The buildings of the institution were scattered among the pines, with the flower beds and well manicured lawns pushing away the wild undergrowth of the northern forest. The men and women of the institution were segregated, each in their own separate buildings, the men being housed in the larger of the two. Spacious sundecks wrapped around the men's building, accessible from all the bedrooms on the first and second floors.

The staff who worked in the institution came from the nearby town, and except for the doctors and psychiatric nurses, were drawn from a blue collar pool. In the summer, university students were hired to cover for the regular staff when they took holidays.

The population of the institution were men and women who were handicapped, or in the language of the day, retarded trainees. The institution was called a Training School. The female attendants were psyche aids and the male staff were white coats.

The white coats in the male building were survivors of a species that became extinct before the emergence of sentient man. These neanderthals routinely subjected the summer psyche aides to what they considered a proper initiation ceremony. If any of the trainees required the application of a cream or ointment to their genital area, the psyche aides were given the task. If the doctor ordered a sitz bath for one of the men, the white coats assigned the job to the newest of the psyche aides.

The white coats also frequently amused themselves at the expense of the trainees. Whenever they discovered

Buddy, a lean, lanky trainee stretched out on the sun deck outside his room, they'd make a deal with him. Because he liked to smoke, but seldom had any cigarettes, he'd do nearly anything for one. More than once he'd be promised a smoke if he jumped off the sun deck to the cement patio below, and he'd have one leg over the railing, poised to spring before any of the white coats would stop him.

On one grim occasion, a pair of scissors were produced, and the white coat negotiated an unbelievable bargain with Buddy: he'd be given a cigarette if he cut off the end of his penis! Buddy was unzipped with his penis in one hand and the scissors in the other when one of the summer psyche aides appeared and demanded to know what was going on.

Occasionally one of the men or women would wander away from the facility into the woods and become lost. Sometimes it was deliberate and they would disappear in pairs. When anyone went missing, another trainee was dispatched to search that person out and bring him back.

One such trainee was Big Eagle, a giant of a man, part Indian, part French. He was fearsome looking, with the heart of a teddy bear. His six and a half foot frame struck fear in the hearts of all the trainees, and he had no difficulty convincing any runaways to return to the institution. His sense of direction was uncanny, and he would thunder through the trees in search of truants, homing in on them as though they were fitted with beepers tuned to his personal frequency.

Big Eagle had a brother who also lived in the Training School. Little Eagle was not as tall, but he was more fearsome looking, and he loved to mimic the ceremonial dances of his Indian ancestors.

On hot Sunday afternoons, families from the nearby town would pile into their vehicles and head north through the pines to the circular drive that wound around the lawns past the main entrance of the Training School. They drove out, hoping to see a work gang of men or women supervised by one or more of the psyche aides or white coats. The activity was termed by the townspeople, "spotting the crazies" or "looking for the loonies."

One such Sunday, a psyche aide and her group of workers were taking a break after weeding the flower beds. They were sprawled on the lawn, cooling themselves in the shade of the massive pines, when a carload of spectators drove by, pointing and jeering. By contrast, the trainees smiled and waved happily as they passed. Several other vehicles approached and the boos and catcalls increased in intensity.

The psyche aide supervising the group became more frustrated and angry with each passing car. Finally, she called Little Eagle over and spoke to him.

"When the next car comes round," she instructed him, "I want you to sit until it reaches us. Then I want you to jump up and do one of your Indian dances for them."

Little Eagle thought it was a fine idea. They waited.

In no time at all, a station wagon came slowly around the circular drive. There were children and adults hanging out of every window, straining to get a look at the loonies. The car moved hesitantly around, until it was opposite the group of trainees lolling on the grass. Suddenly, Little Eagle jumped up and exploded with a blood-curdling screech, arms flailing and legs kicking. Heads and bodies disappeared into the car, windows were hastily rolled up, and away they went down the road like a shot, leaving dust and stones and leaves whirling in their wake. Undaunted, and wanting to finish his performance, Little Eagle gave chase, whooping and waving at the frightened faces pressed against the car windows. Everyone rolled on the grass and roared with laughter. Little Eagle returned through the dust, huffing and puffing and sweating, and asked if he could do it again.

The most memorable Christmas of my life happened in the sixties. The holiday season had always been a joyful family affair, but the recent death of my father fractured my family beyond healing so Christmas was not high on my list of good times. I was an impoverished and struggling university student, so when the opportunity to work during the Christmas break from classes presented itself, I jumped at the chance. During that time I witnessed a Nativity pageant so unique it gave me a perspective towards the holiday season I have never lost. I learned there can be humor in everything, and that knowledge gave me the desire to begin taking life less seriously. The Unholy Angel is an account of that pageant. It was written over thirty years ago with the terminology and perceptions accurate and acceptable for the time.

THE UNHOLY ANGEL
An Institutional Christmas, Circa 1963

Christmas had come to the Training School.

The building was festive with fragrant trees, blinking colored lights in halls, offices, recreation and dining areas. Wreaths of ribbon and holly hung cheerfully on doors and windows.

The dull monotony of everyday life in the institution was suddenly broken. The trainees clamored for the privilege of hanging tinsel and stringing garlands on the trees. Gnarled hands grasped fragile decorations gently, and staff held their breath until they were safely hung on tree branches.

The biggest of the male trainees were engaged in the stringing of crepe streamers on the veranda windows, a task which generally ended in tipping over the ladder and crashing to the floor in a tangle of arms, legs, and brightly colored crepe. The institution staff were caught up in the excitement in spite of themselves, spraying artificial snow on the windows, setting up miniature nativity scenes on coffee tables, hanging Christmas stockings from filing cabinets, and wearing red and white Santa hats during their shifts.

A Christmas concert was in the works, for there is nothing the retarded person likes more than play-acting. One enthusiastic attendant volunteered to help the trainees with a production of the Nativity. A script was hastily written, parts were awarded to the trainees, and rehearsals began immediately in the dining hall with the higher grade trainees co-operating surprisingly well.

The part of Joseph was played by a lean, wiry man with a miserable disposition and a permanent scowl on his face. The biggest and homeliest of the female trainees was given the part of Mary. A fat little man with two thumbs on one hand was an adoring shepherd, as well as an old man with a hump on his back. The three wise men were played by a huge, long-faced Indian, a gentle, affectionate little mongoloid, and a tall, lanky idiot savant who would do anything for a cigarette. Flanking the cradle, which held a cracked and bald Baby Jesus with one eye missing, was a host of angels who were four of the most reliable female trainees.

All in all, the boys and girls of the Training School presented an interesting, dedicated, and almost holy Nativity scene.

The retarded mind learns quickly things that are simple and repetitive, so the dialogue was easily memorized. Like children, retarded people love to sing, so a

Christmas carol was included in the presentation.

As the day for the concert drew near, a feverish excitement gripped the institution. Costumes were made from blankets, sheets, towels and old clothes. A rough stage was built, and in the afternoon of the concert day, a perfect dress rehearsal held the promise of a successful show in the evening. True, Joseph glared angrily at everyone, Mary dropped the Baby Jesus, and the angels sang out of tune, but such minor details did not bother the trainees so they were overlooked.

Excitement mounted as the hour for the concert drew near. There were several seizures early in the evening, and they were recorded as being due to the excitement. At last it was time to go to the dining hall where the players in the Christmas drama were waiting. All were in costume, and even Joseph looked relatively holy with a golden halo bobbing up and down over his head. One angel was bothered momentarily by her wings, but a nurse put them right just as the show was about to start.

And then it was time. Carefully, Joseph, Mary and the shepherds took their places on the stage. The wise men entered, one at a time, presenting their gifts and kneeling in adoration. No one stumbled over lines, tripped over a costume, or dropped a staff or gift.

The angels were just raising their voices in joyous praise to the Christ Child when a piercing voice shot from behind the cradle, "God dammit, I'm off tune! Some son of a bitch tied these wings so fucking tight I can't breath!"

Then an angel swept across the stage, knocking over the cradle, crashing the Baby Jesus to the floor.

"Well, Jeezuz Christ, how the hell am I supposed to sing that damn song when these gawd damn wings are so tight? Who was the dirty bastard who put the damn things on me in the first place?!"

She reached back with strong fingers and plucked at the offending string. One good yank and the wings fell to the floor.

"There," she sighed, "that's one helluva lot better!"

She resumed her position with the other angels, and led them in song. When they were finished, the entire cast received a standing ovation.

The Christmas Concert at the Training School was an unqualified success.

The Seventies

The violence of the sixties produced an uneasy apathy as the world moved through the years of 1970 to 1979. We noted with mild surprise the Watergate crisis and the Patty Hearst kidnapping. The Jonestown massacre sent a ripple of fear through our dulled senses and for an instant we experienced flashbacks of Hitler and his demonic charisma.

Margaret Thatcher became the first woman prime minister in British history, and proved thoroughly capable to the task.

In the world of medicine a landmark was reached: the delivery of the first test tube baby, healthy and physically perfect. And a doctor named Heimlich developed a maneuver that would save countless lives of victims who might otherwise have choked to death on objects or food they attempted to swallow.

Stephen King vaulted to literary fame with enigmatic work, The Stand. He filled over a thousand pages spinning a tale as old as humanity: the struggle between good and evil. One character emerges as an unlikely hero. Tom Cullen is a feebleminded idiot child who is described as "having a goodly chunk of his attic insula-

tion missing." King wrote that throughout history the insane and the retarded were considered to be close to divine. This, apparently, was the basis for Tom's heroic efforts to deliver the forces of good from the depravity of the Walking Dude's army of evil. Tom apparently suffered sudden blackouts, during which he experienced normal thinking and was capable of insightful leaps. Between those lapses, he wandered through the book, a big, lovable giant who spelled all words and names with the same four letters: M O O N.

In Australia in the seventies, a government ban on the word "retarded" gave rise to the enlightened phrase "intellectually handicapped" and we started down the road in search of words that meant the same thing but sounded less derogatory and demeaning. Stephen King listed a number of these interesting phrases in his epic: soft upstairs, running on three wheels, the guy's got a hole in his head and his brain's leaked out, the guy isn't travelling with a full sea bag.

My husband has a brother who is handicapped, and the summer our daughter was four we decided to visit him on our holidays. By curious coincidence he was living in the institution where I worked when I was at university, and I recognized many faces as we drove through the maze of cottages trying to locate his building.

At home we rarely talked about this brother, nor had we ever discussed persons who were physically or mentally handicapped. With the natural curiosity of a four-year-old, our daughter was anxious to see this uncle she had never met.

When I thought back to the summer I had worked at the institution, I remembered visitors being inundated by the trainees who loved to see and touch new, unfamiliar faces. They were especially drawn to children who were frequently overwhelmed and frightened by the attention. I wanted our daughter to enjoy this visit with her uncle, so as we drove through the complex, I attempted to explain to her what might happen when we got out of the car.

"The people who live here with your uncle are a little different than you're used to," I began. "They don't often see children, and they may want to talk to you, and touch your hand or your arm. They're friendly, and they mean no harm. They're just different," I concluded.

"Different how, Mom," she asked, wide-eyed at all the people waving to her as we slowly drove along.

I struggled with this, not wanting to use the words "retard" or "retarded."

"Some of them aren't as smart as you or I. Some of them don't talk as clearly as we, but they're all good people and I want you to be polite to them."

Our daughter waved to a couple of men who were approaching our slow moving vehicle, and I could tell she was considering my inadequate explanation. Then she looked me in the eye, and with the utter clarity of four-year-old logic, she stated, "Oh, Mom, you mean they're mentally handicapped, don't you?"

I nodded my head in amazement and silently wondered why I was trying to explain the concept of mental handicaps to a child who not only understood it, but understood it well enough to use the correct terminology when discussing it instead of the demeaning slang we heard more frequently.

My husband chuckled quietly as I weakly replied, "Yes. They're mentally handicapped."

"And is my Uncle Joe mentally handicapped too?" she questioned.

"Yes," I answered.

"Okay," she said, matter-of-factly, and went back to

grinning and waving at the crowd of men approaching our car.

The Eighties

Early in this decade AIDS was identified and labeled a disease of gays and intravenous drug users. Later in the eighties, it became apparent that AIDS crossed social, gender and age barriers and we were fearful of an epidemic that was thought to be the plague of the twentieth century.

Mount Saint Helen stunned the western world by erupting with phenomenal force, spewing white ash over the land, sending souvenir hunters, seismologists and environmentalists into a frenzy of action. The Titanic was discovered over seventy years after it disappeared into the icy depths of the Atlantic. The American space craft Challenger exploded on takeoff as millions watched live and on television, not understanding what had happened. The nuclear disaster at Chernobyl devastated the land and the people, and the winds over Europe blew deadly with radiation.

Through television we met Benny on LA Law, and Corky on Life Goes On, and even the most skeptical of viewers had to admit that persons who were handicapped could lead relatively normal, useful, interactive lives. Mickey Rooney gave perhaps the greatest performance of his life in the touching true story of a man named Bill who was mentally handicapped. Hopefully, the millions of people who watched the show on television were pulled out of their fear and ignorance of persons who are handicapped, if only for a short while.

In an article published by Reader's Digest, a young mother struggled to come to terms with the birth of her daughter who had Down Syndrome. She felt her child had been created by a genetic mishap. Every cell in her body was different from every cell in yours or mine. She chose to believe that her infant daughter was another biological version of the human species, slower and gentler. She concluded her story with an ironic prediction. Because babies found to have Down Syndrome through fetal testing are being aborted in alarming numbers, her fear was that her daughter may be a member of the last generation of a group silently slated for extinction!

On a breathlessly hot summer afternoon, I sat on our deck, sipping ice cold lemonade, chatting with family members who were visiting on their vacation. Having gotten all the family gossip out of the way we were idly discussing our respective jobs and I launched into several stories of the people in my work place. The men and women I worked beside were mentally handicapped, but they were also dedicated, hardworking and endlessly humorous in their approach to life and its inconsistencies. The stories I told were stories of their successes.

However, my brother-in-law, who had remained on the fringe of the entire conversation, apparently became bored with the subject. He stood up and declared, "I've had enough of this. It's really too bad, Janet, that you can't get a real job working with real people!"

He then stomped off, leaving me open-mouthed and speechless, for the first and only time in my life!

The Nineties

Moving through the last decade of this century, there seems little to be optimistic about. Instead of looking forward to new and exciting things in the twenty-first century, there is a preoccupation with the notion that there will be no life. Environmentalists daily predict gloom and doom because of the ever-widening hole in the ozone, and there is apparently nothing but disaster ahead with the spectre of the greenhouse effect.

Violence and terrorism on a global scale have become a fact of life, and our existence is inextricably connected to computers, for better or for worse. Thus far, the one shining event of the nineties has been the destruction of the Berlin Wall.

Author Dean Koontz gave us The Bad Place, *a spooky tale that straddles the fence between science fiction and psychological thriller. One of the main characters is Thomas, described as possessing a face of cruel genetic destiny and biological tragedy. "He was born with Down Syndrome; his brow was sloped and heavy, his eyelids had an oriental cast, the bridge of his nose was flat, and the rest of his features had those soft, heavy contours often associated with mental retardation."*

Koontz wrote that "liking Down Syndrome victims was not difficult once you got past the pity." Thomas had a friend who considered herself a "high-end moron" and although she liked Thomas, she believed he was a moron as well, not nearly as close to normal as her.

The title of the book sprang from Thomas' greatest fear. He believed the Bad Place wasn't just Hell. It was Death. Hell was a_ bad place, but Death was the_ Bad Place. Death meant everything stopped, went away. All your time ran out. Over. Done. Thomas was telepathic, and the story is skillfully woven around his knowledge of the Bad Thing and his ability to communicate with it. Unfortunately, little can be said about Koontz' sensitivity to and understanding of persons who are mentally handicapped.

Dustin Hoffman's formidable acting skills propel us into the world of autism in the powerful story of The Rainman. We are witness to the puzzling frustration of the person who is autistic. They were once called idiot savants; absolute geniuses in one area, often unable to function in all others. Hoffman's brilliant performance had to start with hours and hours of observing autistic individuals, and we can only hope that his interpretation entertained as well as instructed its audiences.

Garth Brooks entered the music scene with an explosion that rocked the world. Each new song created seismic aftershocks that rippled across the sound waves. He wowed live concert audiences with one spectacular number that had him leaping in and out of a circle of flame. He followed that with a video of the same song telling the story of a high school athlete with Down Syndrome who chose not to compete in the Special Olympics. He wanted to run against competitors who were not handicapped. Garth Brooks' interpretation of a young man's desire to take his place in the world is a sensitive tribute to the courage and strength of spirit within the person who is handicapped.

The couple sat in the doctor's office, stunned and full of disbelief. They had just learned that their son had a severely scarred lung and would have to immediately cease all strenuous activities, including his skiing. In order to survive, he would have to learn to live at a considerably slower pace.

"And that's the good news," the doctor added grimly, as he lowered his eyes and randomly shuffled papers on his desk.

"Sweet Jesus," the woman whispered, and tears formed at the corners of her eyes. "What else?"

"With the condition of your son's lung," the doctor's voice cracked, "it's almost certain that the most time he has left is five years."

The woman covered her face with her hands and cried silently. Her husband leaned close and wrapped his arms around her, struggling against his own tears.

The doctor was an old friend. He waited patiently while the couple clung to each other. He knew they were reaching deep into that wellspring of strength that had never failed them throughout all their son's crises. He wanted to give them some hope to take to their boy. He thought of him, now almost a man, and smiled fondly. In many ways their son was so much more than the average seventeen-year-old.

This young man was a champion skier with the Special Olympics program. Born with Down Syndrome, the world expected nothing of him. But in the world that was his family, he was loved, valued and encouraged to be all that he could be. They helped to shape and develop his competitive spirit when it became obvious he had a talent for skiing. You could see how much he loved it when he was on the slopes. The things that made him different fell away when he pointed his skis and shushed down the mountain. He had medals that testified to his skill, but his parents knew the real reason for his passion. Skiing gave him the freedom and control over his life that he did not have when he wasn't on the mountain.

His mother dried her tears and shook her head, wondering what would happen to him if he couldn't ski.

"There is a chance," the doctor said, softly and hesitantly. Immediately two pairs of eyes, pleading and hopeful, riveted on his face. "A lung transplant would give him more time, and allow him to live as he's used to living."

The woman grasped that thought as if she were drowning and it was a life jacket.

"You mean he could continue to ski?" the urgency in her voice willed the doctor to say yes.

"I believe so," he replied after a long pause, "If he's careful and doesn't overdo it."

The man finally spoke, low, resolutely, and with authority in his voice. "How do we get him a transplant?"

Nine months later, the same man, frustrated, angry and bone weary from doing battle with a system that seemed hopelessly tangled in the red tape of policy, spoke to the media with the same steady authority. "Our son has been denied a transplant because he has Down Syndrome. It's a nightmare. There is no value placed on his life!"

The young man's application for admission to the transplant program had been put on hold because administrators at the hospital, the only one on the prairies where lung transplants could be done, felt they had to develop a policy for Down Syndrome cases.

Their existing policy could rule out transplants for anyone without satisfactory intelligence. And so the young man and his family waited. But while all the policy changing talk was being done, he was running out of time.

In this enlightened decade of the nineties, words like mongoloid, retard, idiot or moron are seldom heard because they are not politically correct. People aren't using those words, but they still seem to be thinking them. Why else would a young athlete have to wait on bureaucratic shuffling and bafflegab to be awarded the same status enjoyed by everyone who isn't handicapped: the status of human being?

3

False Dawn

In the east the sky no longer seems black, rather it is a dark, royal blue. The horizon takes on definition, and the stars are dulled with some even disappearing. The blue pales to gray, and the land is breathless with anticipation, searching for pink fingers of light that reach up from the distant land line. But it is a promise withheld. The sky darkens imperceptibly, not so much seen as sensed. The birds cease their morning songs. There is a hush. The world waits.

This is false dawn. A few seconds of eternity each day when the glory of the advancing light seems reluctantly awaiting the sun's decision to rise.

In the realm of rehabilitation services for persons who are mentally handicapped, we are in the midst of false dawn. The long, dark night is behind us, and although we have light enough to see the direction of our footsteps, the shadows of the lingering darkness prevent us from striding confidently. We move cautiously, awaiting the sunrise.

There are many people who walk with me each day. Each of them is a unique personality with a fascinating story.

Victoria

The aboriginal peoples who were the first inhabitants of North America could neither understand nor explain natural phenomena. Instead, they told stories that combined insight with imagination to satisfy their need to

32

know about the natural wonders they witnessed each day. For example, the blazing ball which gave them warmth and light, whose touch to the land brought forth life and food, they named Sun Mother.

Each time Victoria smiled at me, I was warmed as if touched by the finger of that Sun Mother. Her round, smooth, radiant face was so much a part of my day to day activities, when she wasn't at work I felt as though the sun had decided not to rise.

I sat each morning and watched Victoria walk carefully through the warehouse, as she had been taught, mindful of the fork lift trucks buzzing around her, loading and unloading their trailers. Her progress was slow, but purposeful. There was no hesitation in her step, just caution.

As she drew nearer, and I could see her glorious smile, I would wave to her just to see her eyes crinkle and close with a shyness that was pure innocence. At that point her progress would be halted, because she would turn and present to me her strong broad back. Then she walked backwards, peeking at me over her shoulder once or twice as she moved closer, smiling, always smiling, her face seeming to glow from a light that burned deep within her being.

Once she reached the work area, she would turn and face me full. Each morning, there she stood, immobile for a moment. Then she would stretch her arms wide and say my name. If I were to close my eyes when she spoke, I could imagine her standing at the summit of a mountain, declaring, "I have arrived, I have scaled the heights, I am here!"

That is what I heard in her voice.

"Good morning, Victoria," I would greet her, and every day the impossible happened. Her smile became broader, warmer, more radiant. I would smile back at her. My day had begun. My sun had risen.

Roy

My Uncle Albert was a tall, wiry man who spent his life farming on the windswept prairies. His face was leather brown, wrinkled and grizzled. His stubby whiskers were salt and pepper, and there was always a drop of moisture hanging off the end of his nose. He seemed to walk at an angle, as if he was constantly leaning into the wind. A cigarette dangled from the corner of his mouth, bobbing up and down when he spoke, and his big hands were rough and calloused. It was always a surprise when I saw him without a hat. He had very little hair, and the white of his scalp contrasted sharply with the brown of his face and neck.

The first time I saw Roy, I thought I was looking at my Uncle Albert. Physically, they could have been twins. However, as I came to know Roy better, I realized he and my uncle were quite different.

Roy kept to himself, and spoke very little. One of my colleagues, a newly graduated student, confessed to me that she was a little afraid of him. She thought he was spooky. I thought he was just lonely, and when we ended up working together at a feed mill, I decided to try and breach the wall he had built around himself.

Slowly, cautiously, daily, I ventured into Roy's personal space. There were no words. I just stood by his machine while he worked. Gradually, he became accustomed to my presence. Occasionally I asked if he minded me working beside him. A nod of his head told me yes or no, and I would stay and work, or leave him to his solitude, according to the nod.

Roy was a hard worker, and on hot days the drop on the end of his nose became a waterfall. He seldom slowed his pace, and I began encouraging him with a thumbs up, or a handshake. Gradually, as he allowed me deeper into his space, I spoke to him about his work, commenting on his quality, stamina and dedication. By this time, Roy and I were working side by side nearly every day. We mutually consented to the agreement, and I needed his permission for only one thing: to help him if he was having difficulty with his machine.

One Friday afternoon, after a back-breaking week of hot, sweaty labor, my natural exuberance got the better of me and I gave Roy a big hug instead of a handshake when I thanked him for all his hard work. When I realized what I'd done I was afraid I had overstepped his boundaries. I dropped my arms and quickly backed away. He looked at me gravely, and then a smile tugged at the corners of his mouth. That smile became so broad his ears bobbed and his hat jiggled with its magnitude. Then he snorted nervously.

"I like you, Janet," he declared, and quickly strode off.

That was a number of years ago. Roy and I have worked at many different jobs over the years, side by side, and now it is he who hugs me. He helps his co-workers when they need assistance, he sits with the group during breaks and joins in the conversations, and he tells me at least once a day that he likes me and I am a nice lady.

When I look at Roy now I don't see my Uncle Albert anymore. Roy is his own man, a warm, unique person who tore down the wall he had built around himself, allowing me and others to enter his life.

Gerard

Gerard was a tall drink of water; lean and dark with incredibly striking features. He looked very handsome when dressed in his black trousers and his favorite orange shirt. Even in the drab blue coveralls that were our work uniforms he had an air of authority about him.

There were five of us cleaning animal cages in a research facility, and we all looked very much alike except for our name tags, and whenever a doctor or researcher needed information about the cages they just naturally asked Gerard because he looked like he had all the answers.

Security in the facility was tight because of all the animals and the testing, so as supervisor, I held the only set of keys for my crew of workers. I had been told that Gerard could not manage keys, so every time he needed to use the washroom, I went along to unlock the door. When we were busy, which was always, it was annoying for Gerard and time consuming for me to trot behind him as he strode through the halls to his destination. Finally, out of desperation, I asked him if he wanted to learn to unlock the door himself. He nodded enthusiastically, and his deep, dark eyes seemed to hold a sense of relief.

The washroom key was similar to the others on the ring, but we studied it carefully, discovering its unique patterns and in no time Gerard recognized it with no difficulty.

After much discussion, Gerard and I decided that two weeks was a reasonable time frame to learn this key business. When we began, we found the correct key together, and I showed Gerard how to insert it in the lock with the points up, turn it to the right, open the door, turn the key back to its starting place, and finally, pull it out. I then asked him to put the key ring in his pocket and bring it back to me when he was finished.

The same day, when Gerard asked to go to the washroom a second time, I again went with him. On his own, he located the correct key, inserted and turned it, opened the door, turned it back, removed it, and pocketed the key like he'd been doing it all his life! So much for our two week training schedule. And so much for the information in his file regarding his memory and fine motor skills.

Heady with the knowledge that he no longer needed me to unlock the door for him, he walked taller, worked harder, and smiled broadly each time he came to ask for the keys. Then, of course, we encountered a bug in the system. He returned from the washroom one afternoon and put his hand in his pocket to get my keys.

"Oh, oh," his eyes were stricken. "No keys, Janet," he confessed sadly, and he looked as if his world had come to an end.

"Did you leave them in the washroom, Gerard?" I asked. He shook his head dejectedly, "Gerard left them in the washroom, Janet."

"Well," I said brightly, "let's see if we can solve this. My keys are inside, Gerard." He nodded. "But we need keys to get inside to find my keys, don't we?" He nodded again, more vigorously. "Can you think where we can get another key to open the door?"

Without hesitation, Gerard began naming all the other staff in the facility who had keys to that door.

"Let's go find someone, then," I suggested, and off we went, looking. When we found someone he knew, Gerard explained his problem, borrowed the key, unlocked the washroom door and found my set of keys. We returned the borrowed key and walked back to our work area.

"Now, Gerard," I asked as we resumed our tasks, "if you forget my keys again, how are you going to fix it?"

"Borrow keys," he said confidently, grinning broadly.

I knew he would. And he did. In fact, on one occasion, when he couldn't find any of the staff he knew, he went to the office and asked the Director of the facility if he could borrow his keys!

There are some folk who have the strange notion that persons who are handicapped cannot be traumatized by violent or unusual occurances. By their logic, an individual who is handicapped will feel nothing because he has no perception of right or wrong, good or bad. My friend Gerard taught me that nothing could be further from the truth.

Having no family of his own, Gerard lived with a couple in their thirties. They had no children, and both worked. Ross had a day job with regular hours, and Sally worked shifts. Gerard had lived with them for several years and they seemed to provide the stability he needed.

One day at work Gerard didn't seem to have it all together, so I stayed close because I felt he was struggling with something. Suddenly, he just stopped working and dropped the cage he was holding. When I approached him I saw that he was crying silently, with tears streaming down his cheeks. When I asked if he wanted to talk, he nodded mutely, and I led him away from the noise and clatter to the quiet privacy of the lunch room.

He sat and wept, his lean body trembling violently. My heart broke for him. Gently I asked, "Can you tell me why you are sad?"

"Wrong. Wrong. Wrong." He repeated over and over.

"What's wrong, Gerard?"

The tears flowed harder, and he covered his face with his big hands. "No Sally. No Sally. Ross. No Sally." His voice cracked and he appeared to be in agony.

I tried to make sense of his words. "Are you telling me that Sally has gone somewhere, Gerard?"

He clutched my hand, and squeezed it. "No. Sally work at night. Not home. Gerard home. Ross home. Lady come. Wrong. Wrong. Sally work."

I was afraid of what I thought I was hearing. "Are you saying that while Sally is at work a lady comes to visit Ross?" I desperately hoped I was wrong in my interpretation.

Gerard dropped my hand, gripped the arms of his chair and wailed. "Yes! Yes! Wrong! Wrong!"

I was almost in tears myself, seeing his pain and not being able to ease it. "Did the lady and Ross have coffee and talk?" hoping I was right, but knowing in my heart of hearts what his answer would be.

"No! No!" he choked out. "The lady and Ross. Wrong, Wrong. No Sally." Then he buried his face on my shoulder and sobbed. I wrapped my arms around him and held him until his trembling stopped, and the tears subsided. It seemed like an eternity. Finally he lifted his head and gave me a weak smile.

"Are you alright, Gerard?"

He nodded and smiled again. "Yes, Janet. Gerard okay now. Thanks, Janet."

I didn't know what was happening at Gerard's house, and I had no desire to find out. It seemed that Gerard could not carry the burden of what he saw at home and believed to be wrong. Clearly, he had to share it with someone, and having done that, he was free of the pain and distress he had felt.

Sheldon

When I first met Sheldon, I was actually introduced to the top of his head. That was because he sat, stood and walked with his head lowered, eyes fixed on the floor. He rarely spoke, and on the infrequent occasions when he did, it was in such a soft, low whisper, you had to be sitting on his shoulders or you'd miss hearing what he was saying.

In the beginning, Sheldon and I worked side by side at the feed mill. He usually arrived at work in the morning a couple of minutes before me, and always stood, holding the door open so I could enter first. Each day, as

I stepped into the building I'd say, "Thank you, Sheldon."

We continued this daily ritual for almost a year. Then one morning, I raised my leg and stretched it through the open door frame, exactly as I had been doing for all those months. "Thank you, Sheldon," I intoned, and before my foot lowered and hit the floor, I heard a clear, distinct, loud reply, "You're welcome, ma'am." I became frozen in time with my leg in the air. As I turned my head, my foot finally went down, and I beheld Sheldon grinning at me, eyes dancing with mirth.

After that, more words came, slowly at first, but always with volume and clarity and filled with glee. My assistant, who had an irrepressible sense of mischief, decided Sheldon should learn some colloquial expressions. She first taught him to say, "I am a party animal" which he proved to be true by dancing all night at every party he attended. Then she taught him to tell everyone that "Janet is a foxy lady" and one day she asked him who else was a foxy lady, hoping he would reply with her name. He astonished us both by stating unequivocally, "Mom is a foxy lady!" And having met his mother, I had to agree with him.

Sheldon and I changed jobs together, moving from the dry, dirty atmosphere of the feed mill to the steamy, dirty work area of the cage wash. His incredible strength and stamina immediately became evident. He picked up fifty pound bags of garbage and tossed them into the dumpster like they were filled with helium-inflated balloons.

One of Sheldon's responsibilities was washing down dirty animal cages with a pressure hose spewing hot, steamy water. He was a conscientious worker and did an excellent job of hosing down the hundreds of cages we cleaned each day. But Sheldon's soul was filled with mischief and he had an exuberant sense of humor. As good as he was cleaning the cages, he was diligent and always on target when spraying anyone who wandered into the work area, including doctors, maintenance workers, and once the Director of the facility. And each time he sprayed someone, he had an ear-to-ear grin with an innocent "who me?" expression on his face!

Sheldon's depth of feeling and perception were without limit. I attended a long and emotionally exhausting funeral one morning, and arrived at the cage wash completely drained. Feeling unable to work through the rest of the day, I asked my replacement if she could carry on for me. As I walked down the hall to the exit, my entire body telegraphing my grief and desolation, Sheldon approached me from behind and gently touched my shoulder. I turned, and he quietly enveloped me in a warm, sympathetic embrace.

Not a word was spoken. We simply stood together in that hall for what seemed like an eternity; two people, he comforting me, and I, calmed by the enormous strength of his spirit.

Annie

Her world was devoid of sound.

Never to have heard a meadowlark's song, a cat purring, the boom of thunder, a tinkling music box, children's laughter, the sizzle of bacon, wind whispering through trees; I simply could not begin to imagine a soundless world.

And yet Annie moved through hers each day with an irrepressible spirit and a great deal of noise. Her laughter rang through the work area, unfettered and spontaneous. She vocalized with a high, sing-song stream of sound, and each time she did it I knew she was telling me a story even though no words were formed. Whenever she wanted my attention, she impatiently slapped or banged the table, and if I ignored that or was otherwise occupied, the tone of her voice would change to an urgent command.

Annie spoke quickly and eloquently with sign, and she was an expert at reading body language. I, on the other hand, was a rank amateur with my sign, And she collapsed into helpless laughter each time my fingers failed me. Then she would collect herself, take my hands in hers and move my fingers through the intricate positions of letters and words and together we communicated. My vocabulary started with two signs: "slow" and "in a minute," and I used them most frequently. Annie's fingers flew, but mine felt like I was signing in molasses. She also seemed to sign with an accent. Which is to say she sometimes wanted so desperately to tell a story that her signs tumbled off her fingers half made or abbreviated in the same manner as a person struggling with English will mispronounce words or speak in incomplete sentences.

As eloquent as she was, Annie's spelling left much to be desired. One day, she excitedly told me she was going to blow. I was puzzled and made the sign for again, thinking I had missed something.

Insistently, she signed. "Tonight I am going to blow," finger spelling the last word.

I shook my head and signed that I didn't understand.

Exasperated, Annie touched her chin, furrowed her brow, then looked up at the ceiling for inspiration. This was a regular routine for her, and it always worked. Immediately, she picked up an imaginary ball and hurled it down an imaginary alley and got a strike.

"Bowling!" I shrieked, and then I remembered to sign, "You're going bowling!" Annie bobbed her head up and down in agreement, and once again finger spelled, "blow."

Annie and I shared a curious quality. We saw humor in the misfortunes of the clumsy. I had always justified my reaction to others' clumsiness because I was a class A clutz myself and frequently ended up in the most impossible and sometimes embarrassing situations as a result. But for Annie, it was pure delight watching someone trip themselves on their own shoelace, or open a door in their face.

One day, I was pulling a heavily laden pallet backwards with a pallet jack, a situation that, for me, had the enormous potential for disaster. Straining and grunting, I leaned away from the pallet, slowly putting one foot behind the other, searching blindly for traction. Some sixth sense caused Annie to pause in her labor and watch. One instant my feet were planted firmly on the cement floor, and the next they were flying in the air, propelling me into a summersault. The breath swooshed out of me as I landed splat on my back, narrowly missing the handle of the pallet jack. Annie's glee erupted, and her laughter bounced back and forth off the walls of our work area.

I laid on the floor, red-faced and gasping, pleased that I could provide such fine entertainment for Annie and the rest of the crew, who also found my performance extremely amusing!

Annie had a routine that she worked with everyone she knew. She waited until coffee break or lunch time, and then picked her victim. Placing herself strategically, she would bide her time and watch. Her criterion for choosing a victim was simple. He or she had to have a sandwich, fruit, chocolate bar, or piece of cake. When Annie felt the moment was right, she'd get the person's attention with a tap on the shoulder, or a smack of her hand on the table. Then she would look up to a far corner of the work area, and point a finger in that direction.

Human nature being what it is, the chosen one always looked to the spot she had pointed out, and while that was happening, Annie would deftly hide the chocolate bar or cake or sandwich on her lap, out of site. Then she'd give the whole thing away by giggling uncontrollably while her victim searched for the missing food.

I tried to be sensitive to her needs, and because of that, Annie caught me countless times with her trick.

During the time Annie and I worked side by side, I was overwhelmed by her zest for life. To walk through a silent world, to suffer miscommunication with the inadequate signing of a novice like myself, to be ever watchful of hazards that ears normally give warning of; to do all this and still greet each day with a sense of adventure and discovery is nothing short of miraculous!

Annie's laughter and joie de vivre were gifts, and she shared them freely with anyone willing to take up the challenge of living life to the fullest, as she did.

Jory

Jory was the eldest of several children, and his forthright and self-reliant approach to life was a testimony to the balance his parents were able to find between devotion for their children and realistic expectations of them.

Jory was small in stature, and appeared frail, but he was a man of iron will and determination. He was also pleasant, well-mannered and incredibly conscientious in the work place.

Jory and I labored side by side in a feed mill, bagging and boxing tons of pet food in a work environment that was a study in extremes. Hot in the summer, cold in the winter, we sweated and froze our way through the seasons with never a word of complaint from him.

One frigid January morning I blew into work, propelled by a blizzard that had begun the previous evening and gained momentum throughout the night until it was a screeching, whirling mass of white, blasting anyone who ventured out into it.

Jory was one of eight people who made up my crew at the feed mill. And Jory lived in the extreme north west part of the city. The feed mill was situated in the extreme south east end of the city. Not only did he have to endure a bus ride of over an hour one way to reach work, but Jory also had to walk a good three blocks from the bus stop to the mill itself, and this with a cane to improve his balance.

I didn't really want to be at work on that cold January morning, so my expectation was that none of the crew would make it in. In fact, the only one who did come to work was Jory, wrapped up like a mummy, icicles clinging to his scarf-covered face, red cheeked and blowing steam like a bull ready to charge!

Jory's task was critical to the movement of the assembly line. He had to take a folded box, hold it up to the mouth of the hopper, catch the pre-measured amount of pet food as it was dumped, then put the filled box on a conveyer belt, holding and placing in such a way that the folded bottom remained intact so the food didn't pass through and spill on the floor. The hopper was set at a three second interval which meant that Jory had to have a box at the hopper every three seconds to catch the dump of food. If he missed a dump, the whole assembly line stopped until the mess was cleaned up and the hopper was started up again. Jory never missed a dump, and he performed his task with only one hand!

When we worked with bags instead of boxes, Jory had different responsibilities. He operated the shrink wrapper, a mammoth piece of equipment with a panel of dials and buttons that filled me with terror until I learned their functions and operating sequences. Jory took the operation of that monstrosity in his stride, calmly sitting on his stool, pushing buttons, turning dials, and instructing everyone to keep their hands clear as he shrink-wrapped tons and tons of bagged pet food.

Time passed and I watched Jory become self assured and confident, but I was as unprepared as his parents for the enormous degree of self assurance he acquired.

Apparently in Jory's home, each member of the family had chores they were responsible for. One of Jory's regular jobs was cleaning the refrigerator on Saturday mornings. After several months of work in the feed mill, he simply decided he was going to take Saturdays off. When his mother reminded him that the refrigerator needed to be cleaned, Jory shrugged his shoulders and announced he wasn't going to do it anymore.

Puzzled, his mother asked him why.

His answer was forthright and unequivocal. "I won't be cleaning the refrigerator anymore, because now I have a man's job!"

Delta

If life is a journey, then the roads and highways traveled by Delta were filled with potholes, washouts, and detours.

At the time we met, my own road was rough and plagued with switchbacks; my daughter had moved into adolescence, and an alien life form had apparently possessed her being.

And then Delta's road and mine merged.

It was a noisy confluence: cages clanging in the background, Delta protesting and denying everything with a voice that could easily be considered damaging to the human ear, while I attempted to maintain order and keep everyone working, all the while feeling that I'd never left the battleground at home where my daughter and I daily hacked away at each other.

Delta had been unsuccessful in all of her job placements. It seemed fitting that she make her last stand with us amidst the mountains of animal manure at the cage wash. In the beginning, we were like two she-lions fighting over a kill. We recognized almost immediately that each of us was stubborn, but as we traveled our convoluted path together, it became apparent I was just a hair more stubborn than she.

Weeks went by when there seemed no difference between home and work because both were battlegrounds with an adversary in each camp determined to destroy me. But I stayed on course, flying low and mostly by the seat of my pants. I came to understand the expression, "you don't have to like them, but you gotta love them." I decided I didn't like either Delta or my daughter, but I grudgingly admitted they were both remarkable young women, and I did love them. Why else would I keep going back to the battleground? I saw something in both of them, and I simply refused to give up on either of them.

I read much later that trust is built on consistency. And trust was my goal for Delta. I wanted to show her she could trust me. To that end, and without knowing I was doing exactly the right thing, we sat down together and set boundaries. If she did this, I would do that. It was all very black and white. For every action there was a consequence. It was tough. Very tough. Time and time again, Delta splashed shades of gray on the canvas, and we would stand, not knowing what to do.

Delta had difficulty expressing her feelings. She came

to me one day and said, "I hurt." I looked for a scratch,
or cut, or sign of blood, or a bruise or bump because the
nature of our work resulted in those kinds of injuries.

"Where?" I asked, seeing no evidence of a wound.

"Inside," she replied, with an expression of deep pain
written across her face.

"Do you have a stomach ache, or cramps?" I probed.

"No," she said, "here." And she pointed to her chest.
"I hurt here," she repeated, and patted the area directly
over her heart. I was lost, uncomprehending.

Then she did something completely out of character.
With tears in her eyes, she asked, "Hug?" Immediately,
I wrapped my arms around her and squeezed as tightly
as I could. We stood like that for several minutes, in the
middle of the steam and water and dirty cages and animal waste.

That was the turning point in our relationship. I was
to learn the hurt inside was not a physical pain, but
something much more real to her: aloneness and vulner-
ability. Asking for a hug became Delta's signal to me
that she was feeling lost and insecure, and over time she
learned to wrap her arms around me and squeeze nearly
as tightly as I.

The seed of trust was taking root.

I have always liked to sing while I work, and I do it in
spite of the fact that I can't carry a tune. I'm also a country music fan and one of my favorite entertainers is
Tanya Tucker. I especially like her song, Delta Dawn. It
was a hit the summer after my daughter's birth, and
before she was a year old, every time that song came on
the radio, she would make noises like she was singing
along with it. This only happened when she heard Delta
Dawn, so naturally, I sang along as well.

As the relationship between Delta and I developed,
when I noticed her retreating into one of her funks, I

would break into song, asking her in my fractured style, "Delta Dawn, what's that frown that you have on? Could it be that you're not happy here today?"

At first, it just frustrated her, and she would become angry with me. But I persisted and eventually it became a cue for her to shake off the doldrums and join in the singing. Her singing was worse than mine, so no country duo ever had to worry about competition from us. But we did entertain our co-workers and in the process, developed a bond that allowed us to trust each other implicitly.

When we changed jobs together, Delta and I entered a new phase of our relationship. I knew she could make decisions, she just had never been given the opportunity.

There were safety regulations on the new job that she didn't like. When she began ignoring them, I explained to her she'd be suspended from work if she refused to follow procedures. Delta took a statement like that to be a direct challenge.

"You make me mad," she said, defiance in her eyes and tone of voice. I had the uncomfortable feeling I was talking to the Delta of old.

I shrugged my shoulders. "No, Delta," I explained, "you are choosing to be mad. I am simply telling you the rules of this work place. If you choose to ignore them, I will have to suspend you. If you don't want to go home, you must work within the rules the same as everyone else, including me. What happens next is up to you. Only you can make the choice for yourself."

She watched me and I could almost hear the wheels spinning and whirring inside her head as she sorted out what I had just said. Her struggle to understand was reflected in her eyes. They were dark and confused. Then they lightened up. When her frown disappeared, and she raised her eyebrows in surprise, I knew she had figured it out.

I had given her power. She no longer had to follow my instructions. She could decide for herself what was going to happen in her life. Without actually saying it, I told her I believed she could do it; she could make choices and live with the consequences. And I was right. She took that power I gave her, and proved to herself and to me, over and over, that she could direct the course of events in her life.

Delta and I worked side by side for several years. During our journey together she shed her sullen, argumentative, insecure outer shell, and emerged with a smile and a giggle. She became hard working and sociable; a young woman who felt good about herself, and who was willing to try new tasks and experiences.

Delta was like a time traveler, moving light years from her starting point. Now the highway she travels is straight and smooth, with only a few detours, and no dead ends.

Arthur

When you listen to someone speak who learned English as a second language, it is sometimes difficult to understand what he is saying because of the accent, pronunciation and positioning of the emphasis on individual words. However, if you listen long enough, your ear becomes attuned to that person's way of saying things, and eventually the difficulties evaporate into perfect understanding.

So it was with Arthur and I. His first and only language was English, and he spoke well, but occasionally there were words he couldn't get his tongue around, at least not clearly. But we were both patient, and eventually I came to understand his way of talking.

Arthur was gentle and soft spoken, with graying hair and wrinkles at the corners of his eyes. He always seemed to me old-worldly and aristocratic, and whenever we worked side by side I felt a kind of serenity settle on my soul.

We'd sit and talk as we worked, and Arthur would tell me who he'd seen at the dance on Saturday night, or who was in the pew next to him at church on Sunday morning. We spoke of the visitors to his home, and the shows he watched on television. I would hear about his brother, and his brother's family, and his mother.

Our conversations were soothing and relaxing and I understood everything he said with perfect clarity, my ears somehow censoring out the words he had difficulty saying.

Then I went to work with a crew in the feed mill, and saw Arthur only at social gatherings where there were so many people and so many conversations going on all around us, we really only had time for greetings.

I ran into him at a party years after we had worked together. He was sitting alone, a courtly gentleman, enjoying the music. Wanting to re-experience some of his serenity, I approached him.

His face lit up with recognition as I greeted him, and I knelt down to better hear his soft voice as he spoke. I asked what he had been doing, and he began to tell me, but the music was loud and I couldn't hear him clearly.

I asked him to repeat what he'd said. Again, I could not make out his words. I moved closer, and asked him one more time to repeat himself, embarrassed at my inability to understand him.

He sighed, and spoke the words again.

I simply couldn't get the gist of what he was saying, and then I realized that my ears had lost their ability to sort out the nuances of his speech.

Saddened, I apologized to him, unable to keep the exasperation from my voice, "I'm sorry, Arthur, I just can't make out what you're telling me."

He looked at me and smiled. Then he put his hand on my shoulder and patted it gently as he said, with no trace of frustration, "That's okay, Janet. Don't worry, I understand."

Tom

Most people strive for perfection. Few ever achieve it. There are, perhaps, degrees of perfection some settle for, or perfection in specific areas that are a compromise.

Tom wanted perfection in all things, and his constant frustration was a testimony to his inability to achieve it. He was a small man, with glasses and thinning hair. He dressed immaculately, with everything co-ordinated.

He bore an uncanny resemblance to the Executive Director of our agency, and the two of them also shared a fondness for the companionship of ladies. From a distance, they were difficult to tell apart, especially at social gatherings because they generally conspired to surround themselves with as many females as possible. They were both aware of the comparisons made between the two of them, and laughed about it on more than one occasion.

Tom and I worked side by side at the feed mill, and his penchant for perfection was a source of exasperation for both of us. The boxes had to be folded exactly correctly; the glue machine had to work flawlessly; the shrink wrapper could not buck or jerk; and the taper had to dispense the tape, cut it precisely with no jagged edges, and seal the boxes with absolutely no wrinkles. Because all the equipment was ancient and tempermental, and the finished product generally flawed in some way, Tom spent his days in a constant state of agitation. And when he became agitated, he cursed vehemently, with an endless stream of four-letter words. He didn't shout or spit them out, he paced about and mumbled them. His frustration with the mechanical imperfections we suffered was a daily occurrence, disrupting the flow of the assembly line, so he and I worked together to find a way for him to cope that was more acceptable than walking off and mumbling curses.

When I could see his frustration building, I'd ask him if I could work beside him for a while. Then I'd begin to talk in a rambling way about all the quirks and idiosyncrasies of the equipment and how, because it was so old, we could expect almost anything to go wrong at any time. Perhaps it was the babbling, or the logic in the babbling, but Tom was eventually able to work through his frustration instead of wandering away mumbling curses.

Tom also had a passion for books, something he and I shared. His locker was filled with hardcover volumes of varying subjects and he carried them back and forth from home to work, exchanging them on a regular basis. One morning he came into work with a book nearly as big as he, and explained it was his all-time favorite. I was curious and asked if I could look at it during our break. He seemed pleased at my interest, and reminded me of my request when coffee time arrived. We sat on the loading dock in the morning sun and he opened his treasure. It was an encyclopedic collection of Audubon's bird drawings and paintings. I was astonished! What an incredible book! We spent several days going through it together, page by page, marveling at the detail of the artist, the vibrant colors of the birds, and the sheer magnitude of the volume.

I usually drove Tom to the C-Train station at the end of the day. I'd pull into the Kiss 'N Ride area where all the suburban housewives dropped their husbands off in the mornings, hence the name, Kiss 'N Ride. Each day, Tom would hop out of the car, wave goodbye and trudge off to the train. During our drive from work to the train station, we would chat about work, our families, or things that were happening in our lives. It was a familiar routine enjoyed by both of us. One afternoon after I parked, Tom seemed hesitant to leave the car. He opened the door and backed out awkwardly.

"Bye, Tom, see you in the morning," I said with a wave.

"Uh, sure," he mumbled in reply.

Then, nearly out of the car, he stopped and asked, "Janet?"

"Yes?" I said, puzzled.

Leaning forward into the car, he brought his head close to mine, gave me a quick peck on the cheek, mumbled a hasty goodbye, then scrambled away to catch his train.

I was totally nonplussed for several minutes. Then I noticed I had parked my car immediately beside a huge Kiss 'N Ride sign!

Raymond

Everyone is a book.

Some are wide open, their stories told in an easy, straightforward manner, written in their faces and body language. Some are closed, their secrets refusing to be revealed, book covers forever locked to the curious reader. Some are like nursery rhymes, short, uncomplicated, with clear beginnings and endings.

Others sometimes resemble Russian epics with formidable characters and plots and subplots woven into an impossibly complex pattern, requiring great determination on the part of the reader just to slog through to the end.

Raymond was a Russian novel. I met him first at the feed mill, and he immediately reminded me of a friend who was a truck driver. Raymond stood, defiant, his feet planted with legs slightly apart. One hand tightly gripped a lunch box, the other he raised in a gesture of questionable meaning. His face held a menacing expression. Raymond's round, compact body was clothed in working man's greens; on his feet were cowboy boots; sticking out of his back pocket was a large black wallet, attached to his belt by a long chain.

That first meeting was not fortuitous. Being at the feed mill was not part of Raymond's normal routine and he was not happy. Since it appeared I was the cause of his discomfort, he felt it necessary to vent his displeasure loudly and frequently, constantly reminding me of my responsibility in the matter.

Fortunately, the male dominated atmosphere in the feed mill suited Raymond's temperament. He enjoyed stacking pallets with bags of pet food, then transferring the heavy loads to the warehouse, using the pallet jack to wheel them into position. However, the job was short-lived, and Raymond and I went in separate directions.

Several years later we again found ourselves in the same work environment, and it seemed that the intervening time had changed little. Raymond was still short, and perhaps a little rounder. The dark green work clothes were gone, and he was now color co-ordinated from hat to boots. In his pocket this time was a small wallet with the logo of his favorite hockey team. His lunch box had a similar logo.

His defiant stance and menacing expression were unchanged, as well as his arm and hand gestures, although his vocabulary had grown. And apparently, I was once again responsible for the break in his routine.

We worked this time in a warehouse, replete with truck drivers and fork lift operators. Raymond was content, and gradually we established an uneasy routine punctuated by his occasional one-fingered salutes and pronouncements that I was a cow.

I cautiously peeked into Raymond's book and discovered it was a Russian epic. His moods were explosive and unpredictable. One minute he was dark and brooding; the next, naïve and beguiling. He worked furiously at some tasks, while others bored him to immobility. His pleasure with a job successfully completed was palpable, but frustration was his demon. Lacking the verbal skills to communicate his discouragement, he would clench his fists, tighten and raise his shoulders around his neck, slam his eyes shut and screw up his entire face. Often he was silent, but sometimes a moan of despair would jump out, as if escaping from the depths of his being.

I ached for him whenever it happened, and after it passed, we would sit with our heads together, talking softly, he apologizing, I reassuring.

Gradually, through the gloom in these episodes I began to see a tiny, flickering light. It seemed like a candle flame in a wind, and I tried to provide shelter so it could burn more steadily.

We toiled together in that warehouse, sweating through our physical labor, patiently nurturing Raymond's hesitant inner light. Slowly his book became easier to read. A new facet of his character emerged, one that was happier, friendlier, full of mischief. He talked and laughed with the fork lift operators. He helped his co-workers with heavy, difficult tasks. He hovered around me, and whenever I set my work gloves down, he'd snatch them up and hide them in one of several favored spots, then laugh gleefully as I searched for them.

Between his episodes of pure joy, he managed to

work even harder than before, and his production and quality increased dramatically. At the end of the day he actually appeared disappointed that he had to stop working and go home.

Raymond's light of self assurance became strong enough to show him the way through the shadows of frustration that he encountered. Now the pages of his book read easily, with remarkable characters and a clearly defined plot. No longer is he a tedious Russian novel doomed to languish on a dusty bookshelf. Raymond is on his way to being a best seller.

Max

Max was a thin, bird-like little man whose glasses seemed permanently smeared and smudged, and when I cleaned them for him, I marveled that he was able to see anything at all. When we first met, his vocalizations were high-pitched squeaks. He communicated mostly with hand gestures, facial expressions and body language.

We worked together for four years, and during that time he struggled valiantly with speech, successfully learning to say a dozen or so words, which for him was the equivalent of earning a PhD in communication. We used no formula or therapy or lengthy behavioral program. We just talked to each other, every day that we worked together, for four years. I encouraged his efforts to form words, I gave him my full attention when he did speak, and I celebrated with him when he was able to enunciate clearly enough for me to understand.

He was an odd-looking man, with his coarse black hair twisted around cowlicks and sticking out in several directions at once. He had big ears, practically no teeth, and the eternally smudged glasses, but his personality was warm and attractive, and he was hardworking, good humored and friendly. How could you not like someone like that?

Max had no immediate family, so he lived with distant relatives, a second or third cousin and his wife. It appeared that the care he received was, at best, minimal, and at worst, woefully inadequate. His lunches generally consisted of two slices of bread slapped together with a piece of bologna or sliced ham. There was never any butter, mustard or mayo. That was it. He brought nothing to drink and there was no fruit or dessert. I gave him a cup so he could enjoy the coffee that was provided free of charge to all the workers.

During our regular lunch and coffee breaks, everyone sat around tables, eating, talking, telling jokes, doing essentially the same things as thousands of other people in the work force. Everyone, that is, except Max. He sat apart from us, either on the pallet at his work station, or on the floor. Three times a day, each day that we worked, for close to two years, I invited him to join us. With each invitation he would shake his head, drop his eyes, and huddle with his coffee or sandwich, isolated and alone.

At first I thought he was fearful of the large group of workers, or perhaps shy, but after such a long time, these seemed unlikely explanations. I wondered, then, if he was uncomfortable with the closeness of the tables and chairs, and the prospect of thirteen bodies infringing on his personal space.

The day came when I was just tired of seeing him sitting all alone. I carried my lunch bag down to his work area, and asked if I could join him on his pallet. When he looked at me he appeared apprehensive, but he nodded, "Yes," so I plunked myself down and began eating. After several weeks of sitting with Max, and telling him over and over how we really wanted him to join us at the tables, he left his lonely corner and brought his cup to the table for coffee break.

I was so excited, I dashed out to a nearby bakery and picked up a huge chocolate cake, and when Max joined us again at lunch, we celebrated the event with cake all around, including the fork lift operators and truck drivers!

One day my assistant arrived at work with a large white board mounted on an easel and a bag of dry erasable felt markers. "Found this at a garage sale," she mumbled, "thought maybe the guys might like to draw some pictures, or whatever." She was a woman with a big heart and few words.

"Splendid idea," I agreed, dumping the colored pens on the table. "Okay, everyone," I challenged the crew, "let's see what kind of artists you are!"

We had no idea how popular that white board would be. People printed their names, drew pictures, scribbled, wrote rules for behavior in the work place, expressed joy, anger and frustration on that board. We saw some remarkable things, some so interesting I asked permission of the artist to copy the picture in a journal I kept at work.

Predictably, Max was the last to take pen in hand and work at the board. His drawings were primitive and revealing. One picture in particular, haunted me and seemed to open a small window onto his life.

Max drew a wobbly, but recognizable square in the middle of the board. Inside his square, he put a stick figure with head, body, arms and legs. He added eyes and a mouth on the face. Then he stood back and paused for a moment, as if considering what to draw next. Finally, he made a series of vertical lines from one side of the box to the other. I looked at his picture and got goose bumps on my arms.

Cautiously, I asked him, "Is that a person inside the

box, Max?"

He nodded "Yes."

"Is it a woman?"

He shook his head vigorously.

"So it's a man, then," I concluded.

"Yes," he squeaked. Slowly he reached up and touched the stick figure with his long, bony hand. Then he looked directly at me.

"Man," he said, tapping the board loudly with his fingertips. "Man. Me. Max."

The picture looked to me like a man standing behind a window with bars!

Amazing Gracie

On her first day of work, Gracie walked through the warehouse to our work area like she was the foreman. She thrust out her arm, grasped my hand firmly and shook it, declaring, "I'm Gracie. I'm African-Canadian!"

I smiled as I observed her black, unbelievably curly hair framing a shiny, brown face.

"My mom's black. My dad's white." Her compact, four and a half foot, eighty pound body fairly vibrated with enthusiasm and vitality. Her dark eyes danced, and when she worked she was like a whirling dervish. As I got to know her, I became convinced that when Gracie looked in the mirror, she saw herself as six feet tall. No one ever told her she was short. Or perhaps someone tried, but she was talking at the time, and didn't hear.

Talking was what Gracie did best. Her second best skill was organization. After that, if she had any time or energy, she might actually do some work. At the beginning of each work day, Gracie would organize the crew. She decided who would call the morning coffee break, lunch and the afternoon break. The decision about who announced home time was very important, because that was a status thing. Often, throughout the day, the callers would change, either because Gracie forgot, or we forgot who had been appointed to call what, or she simply decided that things would be different.

The relationship that Gracie and I enjoyed was clearly defined by her, and I was told each morning what she expected of me throughout the day.

"Work today, Janet," she would instruct me. Then wagging her finger at me, she'd continue. "Don't dance. Don't sing. Don't whistle. Don't have any fun. Just work!"

"Okay, Gracie," I'd solemnly reply, then attempt a little soft shoe on my way to the work station.

"Janet! No dancing!" She had eyes on the back of her head. Then she'd reach up, take my arm, and drag me over to my place of work.

"Right, Gracie," I'd say, properly contrite, "just work." And she would smile benevolently, and nod her head.

Need I mention at this point that her instructions were fully justified? I actually spent much of my time each day singing, dancing, whistling, having fun, AND working!

When Gracie was talking, or organizing, or both, her right arm flew around clockwise, her left, counter clockwise. Each day as I watched, I marveled at her timing and co-ordination. Her hands never once smashed into each other. I also half expected her to lift off at any time, and become airborne like a miniature helicopter.

Gracie was a remarkable woman. She had her own language which we called Graciegab. She consistently mixed it into her conversations, guaranteeing that our brain cells would never be idle when we were talking with her.

Our work place had a radio, and by consensus, we

listened to a country and western station. Gracie's singers of choice were Needaneel (Rita McNeil) and Rega Tire (Reba McEntire). Her all-time favorite song was Brinken Hupt by Serious (Achy Breaky Heart by Billy Ray Cyrus).

Gracie was also a hard core hockey fan. Her favorite team was the Dooja Dawbers (New Jersey Devils). She had a hat and jacket with their logo. She came to work one day and announced she'd seen them play the Coopa Tets (Winnipeg Jets) the night before on television.

Once she came to me very agitated. "I had a hackadent," she confided. "I lost my lerkalerk," I had extreme difficulty with this, but after several days of questions, gestures and wild guesses, I determined that she'd had an accident. She'd lost her medic alert bracelet!

Gracie's life was very full. On Thursdays she went to chukka fears (track and field). She also played ball and her team had official oliforms (uniforms). She went regularly to the hess ruster (hair dresser) to get her hair cut.

One morning Gracie announced that she had to leave work early to get her onion assrayed. Jerking my brain cells from their pre-work lethargy, I made a leap and asked, "Are you having a bunion x-rayed?"

"Uh huh," she replied curtly, as her arms revved up for her morning organizational meeting.

Gracie and her family visited an uncle during their holiday. When I asked where this uncle lived, she replied matter-of-factly, "Ice Course."

"Oh," I said, my mind racing, trying to translate. "Does he live close to us, or far away?"

"Far away."

"Did you drive, or fly to see him?"

"We drove."

"Was it a long drive?"

"We drove a long time. All night and all day."

"Did you go east or west?" And I pointed in those directions.

The helicopter arms spun. "We went that way," Gracie replied, and she seemed to lean in a westerly direction.

West. This was progress.

Ice Course. "Does your uncle live in Whitehorse?"

"No."

"Whitecourt?"

"No."

Ice Course. My head began to ache with the effort of trying to solve this puzzle. Then, inspiration!

"Prince George?"

"No."

"Are you sure you went west, Gracie," I asked weakly.

The helicopter arms again went wild. "We went that way," she said, annoyed with my obvious ineptitude.

This time she appeared to be leaning to the east. I was totally defeated. I had not the slightest idea where her uncle lived. Wanting to end the conversation with a little dignity, I asked one final safe question. "Did you enjoy visiting with your uncle?"

"Oh, yes, Janet. He gave me an oomoomboss (granola bar)." That I understood.

But not knowing where Gracie's uncle lived gnawed at me. In the end, I had to call her parents to find out. Her uncle's home was in Swift Current. Ice Course. Go figure.

"I'm wearing my choklut neck sweater tonight at my parents' hasibirthesress," Gracie announced one day at lunch.

I choked on my sandwich. "I beg your pardon."

"I'm wearing my choklut neck sweater to my parents' hasibirthesress!" she repeated indignantly.

One thing at a time, I silently reminded myself, and

my brain shifted into overdrive.

"Choklut neck sweater?" I cautiously asked.

"Yes," Gracie said impatiently. And she gestured up and down her neck with her hands. I pondered for a moment and then the light went on.

"Turtleneck sweater?" I ventured.

"Yes. Choklut neck sweater," she replied, "at my parents' hasibirthesress."

Onward and upward, I mused to myself. "Is this a party you're going to, Gracie?"

"Uh huh," she mumbled, chewing her oomoomboss.

"A party for your mom and dad?"

Her head bobbed up and down.

Inspiration! Anniversary! "It's their anniversary!" I was giddy with success.

"Right, Janet, it's their hasibirthesress," and the helicopter started up as we learned all the details of the party.

A significant event occurred in Gracie's life during the time we worked together in the warehouse. She left her parents' home and moved in with the Holy Ghost. My first thought before attempting to solve this particular riddle was it must, indeed, be an uplifting experience living with the Holy Ghost. Finally, after using the established formula for translating Graciegab, it became clear that her room mates were a couple named Holly and Yost.

Once Gracie had settled in, the three of them went to Holly's parents for supper. The next day Gracie greeted us with her right hand flung out in a grand gesture, palm up, thumb and index finger delicately touching.

"Bone soap," she said expectantly.

"Bone soap?" I repeated with a question mark in my voice.

Again, the sweeping gesture. "Bone soap," she insisted.

"Bone soap," I concluded, convinced there was a vacuum where my brain had once been.

"Bone soap," Gracie said one final time, her gesture almost becoming the familiar helicopter twirl.

"What did you do last night?" I hastily changed the subject, trying to deflect attention from my lack of brain activity.

"We had supper with Holy's mom and dad."

"Oh," I replied absently, toying with the notion that I could be brain-dead.

"And I said, 'Bone soap' to them," Gracie proudly explained, demonstrating her gesture again, this time with both hands.

My mental processes kicked in and the whistles blew and the bells rang. Holly was French. Her parents were French. The French used sweeping hand gestures when they talked.

"Bonjour!" I shouted, waving my arms and startling everyone in the work area. "Holly taught you how to say bonjour to her parents!"

"Right, Janet," Gracie replied. "I said 'bone soap' to them," and for a final time her arm and hand and fingers gestured a gracious 'good day'.

One of our jobs in the work area was moving pallets weighing 500 to 2000 pounds to various locations in the warehouse. We used pallet jacks to accomplish this, and even though Gracie weighed no more than 80 to 85 pounds, she could pump up her load and wheel it around like a dock worker. When she pumped, she often lifted her feet right off the floor, and when she pulled the load, she leaned backwards, her body tilted at a perfect 45 degree angle with the floor. It was a sight that never ceased to fill me with awe. From time to time Gracie would have difficulty with her load, so she'd send me to get a leg crift to do the job. Off I'd go in search of a fork lift to move her load.

During Gracie's employment in the warehouse, another staff person was hired to assist me in the supervision of the crew. Laurie was a highly competent, thoroughly delightful addition to our motley bunch. Gracie was especially drawn to her. She translated Laurie's name into Graciegab and it became Loonie. Later when I reflected on this I decided Gracie must have seen something in Laurie the rest of us missed, because she was, in fact, a little loonie, fitting in perfectly with the rest of us.

If she intended to do what Loonie asked of her, Gracie would say, "Okay, sea hawk (sweetheart)," then go ahead and do it. If she had other plans, Gracie would look at Loonie innocently, smile engagingly, and declare, "I can do that!" Then she'd walk away and do something altogether different.

In the beginning, Loonie had difficulty understanding Graciegab, so I would translate for her. Eventually, her ear became so sensitive to Gracie's way of talking that she translated for me!

Loonie had a unique gift.

She quietly listened and observed and catalogued and filed. Mannerisms and gestures and facial expressions and vocal intonations of the people around her were neatly tucked away in her memory bank to be recalled instantly and acted out flawlessly when she was in a whimsical mood. Her use of this gift was genuine and from the heart. It was imitation born of affection, not the cynical mimicry of an impersonator seeking to entertain an audience. Loonie could swagger or strut, cock her head, look wide-eyed, gesture grandly, giggle gayly, and talk with the same tone or inflection of any of the people in our work area. She so captured the essence of our wonderful co-workers, I sometimes did a double take, not believing what I saw or heard.

As well, Loonie became so proficient at speaking

Graciegab, I often couldn't understand what she and Gracie were talking about.

I believe in immortality. Not of the body, but of the soul, or spirit, if you will. It seems reasonable and logical to me that the human spirit, indefinable but incredibly powerful, has the power to go on and on, making its home one lifetime after another in the perishable bodies of mortal beings. I further believe that some spirits are stronger than others with benevolent or malevolent tendencies. And lastly, I believe in balance.

All these beliefs were crystallized into reality for me one morning as I sat and watched Gracie walk down to our corner of the warehouse. She strode purposefully toward me, her black curls bobbing around her head, and her dark eyes shining. Suddenly, superimposed on her tiny figure, I had the vision of another diminutive presence.

The body structure was decidedly masculine; the hair, white, unruly and flying in all directions. The eyes were deep pools of compassion and intellect. When the mouth moved, the words were clearly heard, but the meaning was obscure because most of us lacked an understanding of them. The walk was hesitant and the manner shy, though an aura of power unmistakably surrounded the figure.

It seemed to me as I watched Gracie that morning that the incredible spirit of Albert Einstein was alive and well in her being. He was a quiet, gentle man whose genius impacted humanity with the explosive dichotomy of positive and destructive energy. He spoke the language of physics, a language that requires great intellect to be understood. And really, what better balance could there possibly be than Einstein's colossal spirit merging with the irrepressible Amazing Gracie?

Dylan

Dylan's path crossed mine in the early days of my rehab career. He was of average height and had a compact, sinewy body. On top of his head was a mop of carrot-orange hair that swirled around numerous cowlicks and refused to be tamed. He had a perpetual bad-hair look. His beard was thick and grew so quickly, that even though he shaved each morning at seven, he had a five o'clock shadow by three in the afternoon. He seemed covered by one enormous freckle, giving him a permanently tanned appearance. But Dylan's most outstanding feature was the color of his eyes. They were a startling green, softened by a gray mist, and they were filled with a sadness that appeared bottomless.

Dylan's entire life was about lonliness, and it was reflected in his eyes. He wanted to be liked, to have friends, to belong somewhere, anywhere. And he wanted these things so desperately, so intensely, that he frightened people. He didn't simply greet you with a handshake and hello, he overwhelmed you by placing himself nose to nose with you, and saying over and over, "My name is Dylan. Will you be my friend? I want to be your friend. I like you. Will you like me? I'm Dylan. I really want to be your friend. Please be my friend. I will be your friend. I like you. Do you like me? Please say that you like Dylan. I want to be your friend. Will you please be my friend. Will you please like me?"

Dylan's need for a relationship was so palpable, so real, so THERE, it was painful. When people backed away from him, or ignored him, or showed fear at his invasion of their space, he reacted in one of two ways. He cried. Or he became angry.

One morning at work, he left the line to get a drink

of water in the lunch room. He was gone so long I became concerned, and went in search of him. He was in the lunch room, sitting at a table, looking at a magazine and crying. He pointed to a picture of several couples in a restaurant, laughing and apparently enjoying themselves.

"I just want a friend," he sobbed, "like the people in the picture."

I took his hand and squeezed it. "I'm your friend, Dylan," and I smiled at him.

I had no idea what a powerful affect my hasty but sincere declaration would have on him. The volume and quality of his work increased. His emotional outbursts all but disappeared. And he did anything I asked him to do on the job. He invited me to supper at his group and I visited him there several times. I met his roommates and house manager. We became true blue buddies.

Less than a year into my rehab career, and only a scant seven months of being Dylan's friend, my manager approached me about doing a presentation at an upcoming rehab conference. Our agency was new to supported employment for persons who were disabled, as was the entire rehab community, and the obvious success my crew enjoyed on the assembly line at the feed mill was something she wanted to crow about. However, I was reluctant to take on the project, not because I feared making a presentation, but because I didn't feel totally competent with rehab terminology. In my heart and soul I knew that my crew was doing marvelous things, and doing them right. I just didn't think I could articulate our success effectively to the trained, educated professionals who would be attending the conference.

Rehab workers speak in a language that is replete

with strings of meaningless letters and abbreviated words. Things like IPP, IF, PDD, PCP, NVCI, AACL, CACL, stimming, b-mod, voc, res and program meant nothing to me, and even after I learned what they were all about I had difficulty using them in context. Let me explain. I worship at the alter of language. I love words. I love writing them. I love speaking them. For me, there is something profoundly physical about clearly enunciating simple and multi-syllable words. The feel of them rolling over my tongue and sliding out is exhilarating. It just seems terribly wrong to fracture the language by speaking with abbreviations or letters instead of words. I studied Russian at university to see if I could wrap my tongue around all those rich, darkly tragic Slavic sounds that were about ninety percent consonants and ten percent vowels. I took a class in Chaucer because I had been told that the professor was a linguist who liked his students to learn to read aloud the Canterbury Tales, as they were written in middle English. I even tried learning Welsh, but failed dismally when it became clear I couldn't hold enough spit on my mouth to adequately spray out the sounds when I attempted to say even the simplest phrases.

When I tried to explain all this to my manager, she stroked my ego by telling me that no one else knew the operation at the feed mill, or the tasks performed by the crew as well as I. Naturally, I agreed to do the presentation. She assured me one of my more learned colleagues would be on hand to translate and assist me if I experienced difficulties. She also suggested I use slides in the presentation, and recruit one of the workers on the crew to talk about the jobs they did on the assembly line.

Of the nine people I supervised, there were only two who had good verbal skills. Dylan was one, and the other was a tall, handsome charming man who had a flatulence problem. He didn't just fart copiously. He farted noxious fumes that were deadly. With a mixture of horror and glee, I could imagine him decimating a roomful of rehab professionals from across the country by ripping one of his toxic-waste killers.

That left Dylan. When I approached him about participating in the presentation, it was as if I had asked him to help me save the world. He seemed gripped by a powerful sense of purpose, and his excitement and enthusiasm were contagious. I knew he could do it. He knew he could do it. But my colleagues were unconvinced. Their reaction puzzled me because I understood we were there to support and encourage the efforts of the people being served by the agency. My manager kept asking me if I was sure I wanted Dylan to help me. I stubbornly insisted he was the right man for the job, and in the end our presentation was well organized, flawlessly delivered, and warmly received by the audience.

I learned that Dylan's passion for words was almost as great as mine, but for him they were a means to an end. He believed this was his shot at that elusive fifteen minutes of fame, and he was going to make the most of it. During our preparation and rehearsals, Dylan saw himself not as a co-presenter at a conference, but as an up and coming celebrity. By the time we actually got to the day of the presentation, he believed there was going to be full media coverage, including television, and he was going to be a star on the six o'clock news. He even offered to sign autographs for his co-workers at the feed mill and his roommates in the group home.

Our agency's need for success in the area of supported employment for persons with disabilities was as great as Dylan's desire for relationships. To that end, management developed a six week training program for job readiness. Because of his performance at the conference, it was believed Dylan was an obvious candidate for the program. Obvious to everyone except me. I agreed that he had potential, but I didn't think he was ready for a placement in a job where he was the only worker who was disabled, and where there would be minimal staff support from the agency. I expressed my reservations, but had only a strong gut feeling to back me up. And I was told, in a condescending tone, that Dylan had been carefully assessed and found to possess all the requirements necessary for admission into the program.

How could I argue? I had no rehab education and only limited experience. Dylan's last day at the feed mill was a sad one for me. I gave him a hug and wished him luck. My heart was heavy and I had a rock in my gut.

Six weeks later I got the news that Dylan had completed the course and graduated with flying colors. My manager could not mask the smug satisfaction in her voice when she told me. I was overjoyed for him, and pleased that I had been proven wrong. However, a month later, Dylan started working in the laundry room of a large nursing home, and three weeks after that he was fired. I had been right after all, but that knowledge gave me no satisfaction.

Dylan couldn't come back to the crew at the feed mill for two reasons. We had hired another worker to take his place on the line. And our agency had a policy that any person leaving one job for another could not return to his previous position, regardless of the circumstances. Period. No matter what.

I didn't see much of Dylan after that, and eventually I learned he had been dropped by the agency because "his needs could not be met." I felt badly for Dylan and lost sleep over the role I had played in his inability to succeed. I did not feel personally accountable for his failure, but I believed I should have fought harder, and argued more eloquently, as my gut dictated, to keep him at the feed mill.

In their zeal for the success of their vocational program, the agency placed Dylan into a situation that was clearly a set-up for failure. Failure for Dylan. The responsibility for what happened rested squarely with the agency. And what did it do about it? It dumped him.

In the aftermath of Dylan's experience, I made a promise to myself. Or rather, to my gut. I decided that no matter who was involved, or what the circumstances were, if my gut told me it wasn't right, I promised to listen, and fight with everything I had for what I believed was in the best interest of the individual to whom I had pledged my support.

Winston

I heard about Winston long before I met him. My daughter worked at the sheltered workshop where Winston spent his days, and she thought he was just about the neatest person in the whole facility.

When first I actually saw Winston he was seated at a table with his lunch spread out, untouched. He stared straight ahead, focusing on something only he could see, with an expression of painful, soul-numbing boredom etched across his patrician features. As I looked at him, I had the immediate gut feeling that this man needed desperately to be somewhere else. I remembered my daughter saying that Winston didn't talk, but he often repeated perfectly words and phrases that were spoken to him. Neither did he smile or laugh, or express sadness or anger. Small wonder, I thought as I watched him. His responses seemed paralyzed, frozen, suspended in time by the dreadful routine of the sheltered workshop.

On an impulse, I found his support worker, and asked if we could give him a two-day trial at my worksite just to see if it would pique his interest in any way. She thought it was a fine idea, and obtained permission from Winston's mother for him to work half days for a week with my crew.

We sorted large pieces of cardboard, stacking them neatly on pallets, tying them, then moving them with a pallet jack to a storage area in the warehouse. Workers had to recognize the difference between good sheets of cardboard and those that were rejected because of holes, tears or dirt. Winston demonstrated his ability to discriminate between good sheets and rejects almost immediately, and I knew he had slipped out of the somnambulistic state I had witnessed at the sheltered workshop. After a week of half days, we decided to extend the trial to two weeks of full days to get a feel for his stamina and task attention.

Winston did so well, he earned himself a permanent position on the crew. He was assigned a locker with his name clearly printed on a bright neon pink circle and the file with all his information was sent to me by his support worker. The thick manila folder was heavy with handwritten formal evaluations, medical information, and notations of a personal and family nature. I deliberately ignored this kind of documentation for as long as I could, believing it was more beneficial to me and the worker if we got to know each other without any preconceived notions about behaviors and family history.

And so, for the first month, Winston and I nervously danced around each other like a shy couple trying out their first waltz together. He stuck out like a sore thumb in the warehouse. He was in his early forties, with a medium build, and dark brown, thinning hair. He stood only an inch or two taller than I, and he dressed like he had just stepped out of the latest issue of Gentleman's Quarterly. He had an aristocratic face with clear, blue eyes that focused on things with such intensity, I was utterly convinced there was a great deal of activity going on inside his handsome head.

After much soul searching, I broke all the rules regarding the violation of personal space and planted myself directly in front of him, almost nose to nose, every day, greeting him, talking to him, teaching him, and above all, telling him I knew that he understood everything that I was saying to him. In the beginning, when he focused those blue eyes on me, they were blank, but before long I saw annoyance, understanding, and amusement, and when I approached him each day, a slow grin would creep across his face.

Winston did everything slowly. I worked beside him each day for six weeks, teaching him, hands on, how to operate the pallet jack. I am not easily discouraged and defeat is not a word I allow in my vocabulary. Long after many of my colleagues have given up on an individual, I push doggedly onward, ignoring the so-called signs that the person I am encouraging is not capable of learning the skill. In one way or another, my persistence is always rewarded.

Winston did not disappoint me. One fine day, when I was otherwise occupied, he wheeled the pallet jack under his sorted load, pumped it up, and pulled it out to the storage area like he had been doing it all his life.

My natural exuberance at his accomplishment spilled over as it has done many times before, and I checked his file for a phone number for his mother so I could call her with the fantastic news. It was my first conversation with her and I was dismayed by her reaction. She did not believe that Winston could do what he had just done.

"But I stood here and watched him," I protested.

"It's not possible," she explained. "Winston's psychiatrist has told us over and over that he is not capable of working at any kind of job. He just hasn't the ability."

"Why not visit the worksite yourself," I invited her, "and see how he works, how he does the job?"

"No, no," she replied, "I don't want to upset him." She was adamant in her refusal, and she dismissed my offer by hanging up on me.

Reluctantly, I got Winston's file out and began to read. A professional who was an expert had given him a life sentence by proclaiming he had autism. For twenty years he languished in a sheltered workshop, making annual visits to a psychiatrist to have the diagnosis reaffirmed so the bleakness in his life could deepen. Any hope his mother might have had for him was systematically destroyed. The notes made by the various support workers who had observed and assessed Winston over the years had characterized her as "difficult."

I began to see why she did not want to hear about Winston's success with the pallet jack. Hope at this stage of their lives could turn out to be a cruel and painful thing after forty years of disappointment.

Fortunately, my own personal job description was written with hope, and I was not about to give up on Winston just because his mother had demons who plagued her. I bided my time, and when it became clear that Winston could sort and stack cardboard consistently, and move it with the pallet jack like a pro, I developed a new goal for him: conversation.

This was very challenging, because Winston parroted everything that was said to him. If I asked him how he was in the morning, he'd look at me intensely and ask me how I was. I'd tell him I was fine, or happy, or tired, or sad, or terrific, depending on how I was feeling, and then I'd explain that I wanted to know if he was happy or sad or tired or terrific. Each time we went through this routine, I maintained eye contact with him, and told him I knew he understood what I was saying and I knew he could talk to me if he chose.

Several weeks into this project, on a busy afternoon, Winston suddenly left his work station, and moving faster than I had ever seen him, headed at a full gallop to the other end of the warehouse. I ran to catch up, and asked him as we rushed together, where he was going.

He turned, and piercing me with eyes full of desperation, he clearly enunciated, "I gotta go peeeeeeeeeee!" I stopped abruptly and watched him charge for the bathroom, then I let out a whoop and fairly flew back to the work area.

I was finally able to convince Winston's mother to come out to the warehouse to see him work, and she was so impressed by what he had accomplished that she dared to have hope. I saw it in her eyes and heard it in her voice when she asked me what I knew about facilitated communication. I explained that I had attended a workshop on the technique, and believed that if it could help a person communicate, it was worth using.

"Win was assessed by a worker at the Society for Autism, and found to be an excellent subject for it," she said. "Would you like to try it with him?"

"Absolutely," I replied, and a week later she delivered a communicator which we could use on a trial basis, free of charge, for a month.

Day after day we struggled with the device. Winston knew how to operate it, but he had decided he only wanted to play. I tried every form of persuasion I knew with the same result each day. Winston would gaze at me with his enigmatic blue eyes and his sly smile, idly fingering the keys, typing out a meaningless stream of letters and numbers.

Feeling defeated and frustrated, I decided to make one final plea. I placed the communicator on the table in front of Winston, and established eye contact with him so he could focus on what I was saying. I told him emphatically, that I knew that he knew what the machine was for, and I knew that he could operate it. I explained that I knew that he knew the machine was there to help people who couldn't talk. Then I said that I also knew he could talk, and I thought perhaps he would rather talk than use the machine. The blue of his eyes deepened and his smile broadened. A quick spurt of adrenalin sent a thrill of excitement through my system, and my next question fairly jumped out at Winston. I spoke carefully, choosing phrases that could not be answered with a simple yes or no.

"Do you want to use this communicator," I asked, locking his eyes with mine, "or do you want to talk to me with your mouth?"

I waited, expectantly. Winston blinked once, and smiled a truly beatific smile.

"Talk," he replied. "I'll talk."

My heart played a symphony as I shut down the communicator and packed it away. The music in my soul continued as I called Winston's mother and told her of his decision. She was stunned and impressed, and commented with a hint of pride in her voice, "If that's what he wants, I guess we'll have to go along with it."

In spite of the fact that Winston was moving forward for the first time in twenty years, I was disappointed by his apparent inability to locate the locker with his name on it. Each morning, in a random fashion, he opened all the lockers except his own, and would just stand with his jacket and lunch bag until I pointed out the circle with his name, "WINSTON" printed on it. It never occurred to me that he knew perfectly well which was his locker but he chose not to acknowledge it for some reason.

About this time I realized that Winston's mother always shortened his name to Win when she addressed him. I asked her if he preferred to be called Win, and she told me that his name had been shortened when he was an infant and since that time he'd been called Win. I thought about this and decided to try something totally unscientific and illogical. I changed the name on Winston's locker to WIN. When he came into work the morning after I made the change, Win went directly to his locker like a bee homing in on a succulent flower. I never called him Winston again, and he smiled broadly each time I addressed him, his eyes saying, with relief, "You finally got it!"

Win's mother called one day and told me they were scheduled for their annual appointment with the psychiatrist, and asked if I would mind going with them. She explained that she wanted me to tell this exalted professional how Win was capable of work, and in fact had been working at the same job for nearly a year. I assured her it would be a pleasure to go along and describe to the doctor the skills Win had mastered, and affirm his value to the rest of the crew and the employer. I looked forward to the encounter with grim determination.

On the morning of the appointment, I was bright-eyed and bushy-tailed, ready to defend Win's newly acquired skills and praise his accomplishments. During the months we had worked side by side, I had observed that whenever Win became frustrated or angry he drew in long, noisy breaths through his nose, then exhaled explosively. The more agitated he became, the louder he breathed.

The meeting began, and so did Win's stereophonic breathing. The esteemed psychiatrist talked about him as if he wasn't there. It was all very clinical and impersonal. He refused to acknowledge that Win was able to learn specific work skills, then use those skills on a daily basis. The fact that I witnessed the glory of Win's accomplishments each day failed to impress him. He flatly refused to believe anything I told him. I began to breathe as noisily as Win.

Talking to Win directly, with full eye contact, I asked him to tell the doctor what sort of work he did.

"Sort paper," he said proudly.

"Do you like your job?" I asked.

"Yes." He grinned broadly.

"Would you like to go back to the sheltered workshop?"

"No." Win shook his head emphatically.

The doctor interrupted. "Do you like working?"

Win drew in a long, noisy breath. "Yes."

The doctor continued. "Do you like drinking coffee?"

"Yes."

"Do you like watching television?"

"Yes."

"Do you like flying to the moon?"

"Yes."

"Do you want some lunch?"

"Yes."

"Do you want to change jobs?"

"Yes."

"Do you want to go back to the sheltered workshop?"

"Yes."

The psychiatrist gave me a smug look and shrugged his shoulders. "He doesn't know what he wants. He's incapable of making decisions. He can't learn anything. He can't work."

And then he dismissed us with a wave of his hand. We walked down the hall toward the door, and it seemed to me that the walls were contracting and expanding with the force of Win's thunderous inhaling and exhaling. Then, miraculously, when we exited the building, Win commenced to breathe normally.

"You don't like him, do you, Win," I said, stating the obvious.

He looked at me, and a grin sculpted his face into a picture of relief. "No." And then he sighed. "Work?" he asked, hopefully.

"You bet, Win, we'll go back to work. Back where you're needed because you do such a good job."

Win stood taller and puffed out his chest proudly.

I tried to reassure his mother. "We know he can work. He knows he can work. And most importantly, his employer knows he can work. That's what counts."

Win is still at the same job, everyday doing what his psychiatrist says he's incapable of. I wonder sometimes, who is more disabled, he or Win.

Angelo

Angelo was a short, rotund man with glasses, thinning hair, an engaging smile and dentures that didn't fit. He tried to keep his teeth in place with Polygrip, and I believe he must have purchased that product by the truckload because every morning he flashed me a magnificent Polygrip grin with bits of pink overflowing onto his teeth, clinging to his lips and chin, and trailing behind him on the floor.

In reality, the Polygrip was an exercise in futility because each day, before our morning break, Angelo yanked out his dentures with a flurry of pink, and placed them in the back pockets of his jeans.

Angelo wore his glasses jammed tight against the bridge of his nose, perhaps to make up for the looseness of his teeth. The wire frames appeared melded to his skin, and in all the time I knew Angelo, I never saw him take his glasses off.

The most curious thing about Angelo was his jeans. He wore them pulled up so high over his portly middle that his belt rode halfway between his waist and armpits. This naturally exposed his ankles so he appeared to be wearing flood pants. He reminded me of Tweedledum and Tweedledee from Alice In Wonderland. But the thing that made Angelo unique among the workers was not just his jeans. Or the way he wore his jeans. It was what happened to his jeans each day after he had been working for a while.

I observed him one morning, making his way down the warehouse in the direction of the bathroom. He was walking in a very odd manner.

"What on earth is he doing?" I wondered out loud.

Loonie had also seen him, and she suppressed a grin and replied, "I think he's trying to liberate the family jewels."

"What?!?" I couldn't believe my ears.

She giggled. "Well, Janet! Just look at how he's moving, then tell me why he's moving that way!"

I did. And Loonie was right.

Angelo took three or four steps, then stopped. He lifted one leg about six inches off the floor, stretched it out in front of him, pointed his toes, and then balancing on his other foot, he gave his ample behind a vigorous shake. Then he took a few more steps, stopped, and did it again, reversing his legs. It was quite a performance.

I thought about it, and I concluded that with all the bending and twisting he did on the job, and wearing his jeans so high around his middle, it was natural to expect that certain things would become somewhat pinched and constricted.

I watched Angelo shuffle and wiggle and shake his way down to the bathroom, torn between feeling empathy for his predicament, and finding his unique footwork and body moves absolutely hilarious. He went through this routine several times a day, and it finally just got to be too much for me. I was talking to one of the warehouse employees who drove a fork lift one afternoon when Angelo jiggled by, stopped, pointed and shook.

The fork lift driver and I watched him, and then he asked, "What the hell is he up to?"

Barely able to contain my laughter, I managed to say, in a strangled voice, "Angelo is doing what we call the Testicle Shimmy!"

The man looked at me with a puzzled expression. I struggled against my erupting giggles. "The Testicle Shimmy! Think about it!" And then I was gone, collapsed on the floor of the warehouse, guffawing uncontrollably, and nearly wetting myself in the process.

Loonie and I tried, over and over, to convince Angelo that he would be more comfortable working if he wore his jeans lower on his waist. But he would have none of it. And so, for the rest of the time that he worked in the warehouse, Angelo entertained us frequently throughout the day with his fancy footwork and herky-jerky dance.

4

Sunrise

A sunrise is about beginnings. It can be bright and rosy and filled with promise. Or it may be gray and gloomy and heavy with foreboding. But it is there, every morning, giving us another chance, a clean slate. Each day we inherit the gift of being able to set aside the mistakes of yesterday and begin anew.

Human nature being what it is, we are likely to repeat our mistakes, or commit even greater ones, but the opportunity does exist for us to learn from our errors and use that wisdom on another new day.

In the world of rehabilitation, a sunrise is also about progress and change. A parent once told me that she believed her daughter, who was disabled, had come a very long way. But, she pointed out, there was still a great distance to go. The daughter's progress was slow because she was taking baby steps. It appears, at times, we are all taking baby steps, and many days it is one step forward and two back. But this is progress. A few short years ago we were taking one step forward and five back!

As we try to see through the brilliance of the sunrise into the future, three final stories need telling. Two come from the long dark night, and one belongs to the sunrise. If we are ever to take more than baby steps, we must first deal with the messages in these stories. The thread that connects them all is the omnipresent abuse against persons who are disabled.

85

That the first story did or did not happen is unimportant. I have heard it several times since those long ago summers when I was a student working in an institution. Myth or truth, the meat of the story is real and chilling.

The second story occurred in a place where I worked, and was told to me by one who watched it unfold. Whenever I think of this story I am reminded of the fact that truth is stranger than fiction.

The final story occurred recently and involves people I know well. It is a poignant and revealing portrayal of one man's struggle to cope with changes that he is ill-equipped to handle.

The Mongoloid Myth

The man was a mongoloid of undetermined age and origin. Heeding well-meaning advice, his mother had placed him in an institution shortly after his birth, and forgotten he even existed.

Life from his earliest memories had been programmed and conditioned for predictable behavior, actions and responses. He was an excellent subject for the institutional way because mongoloids were known to be ritualistic and non-aggressive by nature. In fact, most of them were compliant and quite affectionate, and he was no exception.

The place he called home was a large, sprawling structure built a considerable distance from the houses and streets of normal folk, and although he could find his way through the maze of halls and stairs and dining rooms and workshops and dormitories, he was unfamiliar with the grounds and surrounding countryside.

One glorious fall day, lured by the warm sun and

autumn colors, he wandered away from the building and became lost. His absence went unnoticed until nightfall when a bed count was taken, but by then it was too cold and dark to begin looking for him. In the morning he had still not returned, so a search party of staff and trusted trainees began combing the woods adjacent to the institution. On the second day of the search they found him.

Apparently, as night fell, he did what he had been programmed to do. He removed his clothes, folded them neatly, and set them in a tidy pile on the dead leaves that carpeted the ground in the woods. He then lay down with his clothing at his feet, and curled himself into a ball. He went to sleep and died of exposure that chilly autumn night. When the searchers found him, his body and clothing were a sad, silent testimony to the effectiveness of the conditioning imposed upon him throughout his life.

This story identifies the most insidious type of abuse against persons who are disabled. It involved the institutionalization of individuals with the belief that programming their daily lives would avoid any inappropriate or bizarre behaviors. Residents became locked into routines and systems that robbed them of individuality, reducing them to automatons with no ability to function beyond the confines of the institution. In reality, institutionalization made it easier for the staff to control the residents. It was also advantageous for the staff because rules and consequences were clearly defined with little or no need to make decisions or take responsibility for actions that in a more enlightened age might be viewed as negative or abusive.

Saturday's Child

There is a rhyme that tells the days of the week, and what a person born on each day can expect from life. It says that Saturday's child has to work for a living.

It is not known on which day Philip was born, but he was certainly made for work. He was a bull of a man, not tall, but solidly built. Broad shoulders. Thick, muscular legs and arms, and massive laborer's hands that could work all day and in the evening follow songs on the radio, making music with a couple of spoons borrowed from the kitchen. He had a square jaw, broad nose, and wide set eyes sunk under a prominent brow. In the middle of his forehead was a huge rock-hard callous built up from years of banging his head against pipes, walls, doors, bath tubs, whatever solid object he could find when he became agitated and went up the pole.

He was an agreeable man who liked to sneak up behind and give bone-bruising bear hugs to his favorite people. For all his strength he had a gentle spirit, and was really only a danger to himself and inanimate objects when he couldn't cope.

But Philip's most outstanding feature was none of these, and it was only outstanding in the minds of those who were envious. He was endowed with a penis that hung, flaccid, nearly to his knees. It was nothing to Philip because he had lived with it all his life, but it was a constant source of amusement to all the male staff, called white coats, who encouraged him to parade around in his night shirt, which barely covered his buttocks. Their encouragement, naturally, became more raucous when any of the female staff were working in the area.

One such female staff person was a young university student, employed for the summer to provide coverage for holidays. Her name was Susan, and little was known about her because she was not a local girl. She had rented a little house in town, lived alone, and kept to herself. She was tall and muscular, with long, sun blond hair, clear blue eyes and classic girl-next-door features.

Susan was, indeed, a woman way ahead of her time. In an era when Gloria Steinem was still a virgin trying to find herself on some university campus, Susan knew exactly what she wanted. She knew where to get, and she boldly went after it.

On her first day of work the testosterone levels at the institution rose dramatically and the white coats stood around gawking and drooling. Three days into her first week, they began swapping fantasies about her, and by the end of the second week, all had approached her and asked for a date. She firmly and courteously turned them all down.

In that situation, the sophisticated male of the nineties might assume Susan was a lesbian and let it go at that. No so with the men of the sixties. They were super studs; chauvinistic kings who believed they were God's gift to humanity in general and women in particular, and it was obvious to them Susan hadn't figured things out yet. But they could afford to wait. She'd come around eventually. They all did.

While they waited, they got Philip to strut in his night shirt, and invited Susan to view what their puerile minds called "the splendor of his member."

Apparently, Susan was impressed, and made several discreet inquiries. She learned that the institution had a loose policy allowing staff to take trainees out for a day at a time to do odd jobs of their choosing. All they needed to provide was transportation, a meal, and whatever pay seemed appropriate to the task.

Susan's small rented house sat on a large lot with an

expanse of lawn, flowers, shrubs and garden area that needed tending. Philip seemed up to the job, so they agreed to a weekly Saturday commitment.

The white coats knocked themselves out for half the summer trying to persuade Susan to date one of them before they found out about the Saturday arrangement she had with Philip. After much speculation and more wild fantasizing, they finally dragged Philip into the linen room and grilled him.

"What do you do when you go to Susan's house on Saturdays?"

"Mow the lawn."

"Anything else?"

"Weed the flowers."

"And?"

"Trim the bushes."

"And?"

"Hoe the garden."

"Anything else?"

"Susan makes lunch and we eat it."

"What happens in the afternoon?"

"Sometimes I work outside some more if I'm not finished."

"And if you're finished?"

"Then we go into her bedroom and go to bed."

Grunting and sweating in the crowded linen room, the white coats continued their questions, knowing what the answers were, but needing to hear them spoken.

"What do you do then?"

Philip eyed them suspiciously. "You don't know what people do in bed?"

"Well, yeah, but what do you and Susan do in bed?" They leered at him.

He shrugged his shoulders, bored with the questions. "You know. What do you do with a girl in bed?" Then he turned and walked out of the stifling little room, leaving the white coats glassy-eyed and panting.

At the end of the summer Susan went back to university. After a time, it seemed as if she'd never been there. Philip continued to bear hug his favorite people and play the spoons in the evenings. The white coats never did figure out why a woman like Susan preferred a stupid retard even if he did have a ten-inch dick when she could have had any or all of them!

This story describes with gut-wrenching realism the flagrant exploitation of persons who are disabled by their so-called care-givers. The most disturbing aspect of this particular episode is that none of the players who were not disabled believed they were doing anything wrong. In fact, the only person who displayed a measure of humanity and decency was the victim, who refused to be drawn into the care-givers adolescent braggadocio of real or imagined sexual conquests.

RVs and Power Rangers

Maury's history was unremarkable and strikingly similar to many of the persons who were born with a disability thirty or forty years ago. Maury had Down Syndrome. His youth was spent in an institution where his life was completely structured, following a rigid daily routine.

The first major change in Maury's life occurred when the institution was emptied, and he moved into a group home. As it turned out things changed little for Maury, because group homes were nothing more than miniature versions of the institution. The daily activities were subject to the whims of the group home manager.and her staff. With an incredible turnover rate in residential services, Maury seldom knew if he was coming or going because each new manager changed the routines and rules according to her training, experience and personal preferences.

Maury had a gentle, affectionate nature. His passion was vehicles, specifically recreation vehicles. He filled his pockets with pictures of trucks, vans, campers and motor homes. He spent hours with black fingers, thumbing through pages and pages of pictures.

Change is never easy, but when it occurs swiftly, and when it affects every aspect of one's life, it is difficult, if not impossible to move through it without suffering some kind of trauma or damage.

It seems this was the case with Maury. Group homes were closed and residents were placed in private homes with families. As well, rehab service providers began focussing on two concepts: choice and inclusion.

Suddenly, Maury's relatively placid life hit a stretch of turbulent white water. His father, with whom he had enjoyed a close, long term relationship, married after many years as a widower. Mutual animosity between Maury and his father's wife developed quickly. At the same time, his group home closed and Maury was placed with a family who had absolutely no experience or knowledge of persons who are handicapped. They received orientation which stressed choices for the clients. Their interpretation allowed Maury the freedom to do whatever he chose.

Maury may have been handicapped, but he wasn't stupid. He figured things out very quickly. He could go to bed when he wanted. He could eat what he wanted. He didn't have to be at work on time, if he chose to go at all. He never liked shaving, so he just stopped doing it. The same was true of showering. The constraints of a lifetime were suddenly gone!

Maury became glued to the television set, and as a result, lost interest in his RV pictures. Then he discovered the Power Rangers, a children's show featuring superhuman adolescents who ran around in space-type suits, vanquishing evil villains with karate chops, kick boxing, back flips, choke holds and running leaps.

Maury's pockets soon bulged with pictures of his Power Ranger heroes. He intently watched them, and practised their moves at every opportunity. Over time his co-ordination improved, he became physically stronger, and was more fit that he'd ever been.

There were other changes that were disturbing to those who knew Maury well. Because he chose not to shave or shower, or even bath with any regularity, his physical appearance deteriorated, and he actually began to look and smell like a bum. He was frequently late for work, and when he did show up, he often chose to do nothing, except practice his Power Ranger moves.

But it was the subtle changes in his character and personality that caused the greatest concern. Gone was the smiling, friendly Maury. He became sullen and argumentative. Every move and gesture had aggressive undertones. His eyes were dark and menacing, and his facial expressions, haughty and defiant.

One day, his work supervisor asked him to stop showing her his collection of Power Ranger pictures, explaining she was tired of it, and she didn't like looking at them.

He stomped off in a huff, waving his arms wildly, kicking the chairs and lockers in his path. Later, he approached the supervisor who was talking to another staff. He walked behind her and when he was directly opposite her, he shot his arm out and gave her a Power Ranger punch right between the shoulder blades. The blow was so quick and forceful that it snapped her head back, cracking her neck. He had acutally given her whiplash. She instantly had a blistering headache, and her neck and shoulders ached and throbbed for several days.

Maury went home with the story that his supervisor had hit him. He was not disciplined in any way for his actions, nor did he suffer any negative consequences over the incident.

His supervisor, on the other hand, was questioned by several levels of management, whose primary concern was whether or not there was a witness to the so-called assault. Incredibly, they seemed reluctant to believe her, but were eager to give Maury the benefit of doubt!

This story illustrates the disastrous effects of what I call abuse by omission.

Consider the result of turning a small child loose, with no constraints, in a candy shop. Similarly, what might the outcome be if a homeless vagrant was given one million dollars cash. The child would eat candy until he became physically ill. The vagrant might either squander his money until it was all gone, or be beaten senseless by his fellow vagrants and have his new-found fortune stolen from him.

If the person who is disabled is going to have the power of choice, he must first learn how to choose, and what to expect in the matter of consequences once he has chosen one course of action over another. Choice involves decision making and problem solving. These are skills that have to be learned. They are not inherent or instinctive. To give choice to an individual without including the tools for making choices is irresponsible, and ultimately sets him up for failure.

5

Us and Them

Whenever there are discussions involving people who are handicapped, the conversation is about US and THEM. It has always been that way.

Inclusion, the current buzz word in rehab circles, will never be a reality as long as there is US and THEM!

I believe that we are all just people, irregular people, if you wish, who are working together to realize our individual potentials and dreams. We are partners in this endeavor. We don't necessarily have to be in agreement, and we don't have to like everyone, but we do have to live and work side by side.

I am the only child of middle-aged parents. My mother had a full time career. At home she was both physically and verbally abusive towards me. By contrast, my father was over-indulgent. I grew up left-handed in an age that considered this to be deviant behavior. I am clumsy and for most of my life I have been painfully shy. I've worn glasses since childhood and have a condition which will ultimately cause blindness in my left eye. In school I was an incredibly average student who needed a tutor to get through algebra, geometry/trigonometry and physics. I attended university, but was kicked out because of an attitude problem. I hold no certificate, diploma, or degree from any post secondary learning institution. I have no formal or specialized training in anything. Am I any less handicapped than those people whose stories you just read? Whose life has greater value?

It's been said that life is not about living forever. Rather it's about making the journey worthwhile. I have journeyed with the people whose stories I have told, and they have made my life worthwhile. They taught me about patience and laughter, frustration and anger, fear, despair and joy. But my greatest lesson was courage. I discovered there is a well-spring of courage deep in each of the remarkable people it's been my privilege to know, and they draw on it daily. They have shared their courage with each other and with me, and I believe there is nothing they can't do because I know what they have already done.

I would like to salute their successes and offer my gratitude for their friendship with the Irregular Peoples' Creed, which I write and dedicate to irregular people everywhere.

Irregular Peoples' Creed

I AM SPECIAL.

There is not another single person in the world
who is like me.
No one looks as I do, thinks as I do.
No one laughs quite like me, or laughs at the
same things as me.
That which causes me joy or sorrow does not affect
anyone else in exactly the same way.
Nowhere is there anyone who shares my taste
in books or music.
There are tasks I enjoy that others find boring or
insignificant, and while many will do things better
than I, no one will do them precisely as I.

I AM ONE OF A KIND.

The configuration of my being: my eyes, my hair, my
body; all these factors combine to make me an
individual, a unique part of God's plan.
He created me to do a special job, one that
no one else can do.
He gave me a combination of talents and characteristics
that will never again be duplicated in all of eternity.
The task he has chosen for me is like none other in the
world, and only I can do it.

I AM UNIQUE.

Only my eyes see a particular beauty in the swirling
snow of a blizzard; only my ears hear a symphony
when thunder rolls across the heavens.
No other being feels pain in the same way as I; no one
has daydreams like mine; no one can curl their lips
around a smile the way I can.
When I raise my voice in song, it may not be as clear or
pure as other voices, but it comes from my soul,
and no one else knows the words or tune.

I AM DIFFERENT.

Most of the time I like me as I am.
When I become disappointed in me, and I look for
ways to make changes, I must remember that God
intended me to be this way; to have imperfections
and doubts and fears.
They are all part of my differentness.
If I COULD change anything, it would be to increase
my understanding of my differentness, and the
differentness of every other being in the world.

I AM SPECIAL.

MEMBRE DU GROUPE SCABRINI

Québec, Canada
2000